## PUFFIN BOOKS

### The Wacky World of Wesley Baker

Gene Kemp grew up near Tamworth in the Midlands, took a degree at Exeter University, taught, married and had three children. She is best known for her Cricklepit School stories, which include *The Turbulent Term of Tyke Tiler* (winner of the Carnegie Medal and the Other Award), *Gowie Corby Plays Chicken*, *Charlie Lewis Plays for Time* (runner-up for the Whitbread Award 1985) and *Just Ferret* (runner-up for the Smarties Award in 1990). In addition are *The Clock Tower Ghost, Jason Bodger and the Priory Ghost, Juniper*, short stories, a poetry anthology, and writings for TV and radio. In 1984 Gene Kemp was awarded an honorary degree for her books, which have been translated into numerous languages.

Gene Kemp lives in Exeter with an elderly, evil-tempered cat and a lot of wildlife. Her hobbies include reading as much as possible, watching TV, exploring Dartmoor, supporting Aston Villa and Exeter, playing with her grandchildren and doing nothing.

Gene Kemp

# The Wacky World of Wesley Baker

Illustrated by Chris Fisher

PUFFIN BOOKS

PUFFIN BOOKS

Published by the Penguin Group
Penguin Books Ltd, 27 Wrights Lane, London W8 5TZ, England
Penguin Books USA Inc., 375 Hudson Street, New York, New York 10014, USA
Penguin Books Australia Ltd, Ringwood, Victoria, Australia
Penguin Books Canada Ltd, 10 Alcorn Avenue, Toronto, Ontario, Canada M4V 3B2
Penguin Books (NZ) Ltd, 182–190 Wairau Road, Auckland 10, New Zealand

Penguin Books Ltd, Registered Offices:  Harmondsworth, Middlesex, England

First published by Viking 1994
Published in Puffin Books 1995
1 3 5 7 9 10 8 6 4 2

Filmset in Ehrhardt MT

Made and printed in England by Clays Ltd, St Ives plc

# Chapter One

As Agnes Potter Higgins crashed through the classroom door, I thinned myself back behind Dino, the gynormous papier mâché dinosaur that my friend Kevin and I made last term. I wanted to read Kev's *Beano* in peace, and the last thing I needed was Agnes Potter Higgins explaining the jokes. But even leaning right back I could still see her as she lifted her nose and sniffed the air like a tracker dog, her bat-like baby-blue peepers blinking behind her revolting specs decorated with pink teddy bears. I panicked a bit. Could she really sniff me out? I'm pretty neurotic about smells just now, especially as Simon Partington keeps singing about the scent of roses whenever I go near him, which I try not to. He always overkills jokes.

You may wonder why I'm hiding from Agnes Potter Higgins. And why I'm neurotic about smells.

Well, you see, I hate her. She's been in my class for yonks and I never noticed her much, just a moody show-off girl, a pain in the neck. But starting last week she decided she loves me. And since then my life has turned into a horror film.

She draws hearts with my initials and hers in them. She sends me love letters by the sackful.

She puts chocolates and bath salts on my desk. Well, the chocs are fine. I shared them with Kevin, Carly Baker and Tim Waring, but the BATH SALTS! You can guess how I suffered. Simon Partington held his nose every time he got near me. He would. *That's* why I'm neurotic about smells.

She blows kisses at me. Can you imagine it? I can't bear it. Her mother offers me lifts in their clapped-out old car so full of nodding dogs that she can't see properly and runs into things all the time. I never accept (the offers) because it's a health hazard, that car, and besides, it's always full of the Horrible Potter Higgins Sisters: Sophie, Tryphena, Melody and Agnes. Yuk.

And right now she's all smiles and sunshine, but if I don't do what she wants – be her boyfriend, yuk – the thunderclouds will gather and I'll be struck by lightning. Help!

'You see, she's got a split personality,' I told Kevin, who's not as stupid as he looks. No one could be as stupid as *he* looks.

'Not split. Splatted,' he said, and ran off to play football. He's always running off to play football. That was last week.

*This* Monday morning, as I said, I flattened my back against the wall – it's a good job I'm skinny – as Agnes looked over the classroom. There's a school uniform, but that's not for Agnes Potter Higgins. Oh, no, she was rigged out in purple cord pantaloon things with lace dribbling over them, green earrings and BIG, but COLOSSUS-BIG, very old trainers.

'Mummy thinks clothes should express our personalities,' she'd told Mr le Tissier at the beginning of term, explaining why she wouldn't be wearing grey and navy.

'Wezzie,' she trilled, rising to a high screech like a dentist's drill. 'I know you're there, Wezzie. It's no use hiding from me. Come on out. I want you. Agnes wants you, Wezzie.'

'We know. Everybody knows Agnes loves Wezzie. Agnes wants Wezzie,' sang out Carly Baker, the class know-all.

'Save me,' I squirmed, shrivelling inside.

Most of my friends joined in the chorus with Carly. With friends like these, who needs enemies? Kev unpeeled me gradually off the wall and tried to pull me out of my safe place. I grabbed Dino the dinosaur, who'd started life off as *Tyrannosaurus rex* but hadn't been able to keep it up. He had collapsed into Dino the dinosaur with a weak neck (the bit Kevin worked on).

'Wezzie doesn't love Agnes, ooh, oooh, ooooh, sad,' warbled Carly.

Kevin pulled me. I clung to Dino. The neck gave way and we rolled together on the floor, bits of papier mâché falling like dirty snow.

Something hitting my nose made me open my eyes to find Agnes bending over me so close that one dangling earring was in my nostril.

'Wezzie, are you hurt? Wezzie, I've got to talk to you. Wezzie, are you hurt? Speak to me, Wezzie.'

'Gerroff,' I spluttered, struggling and pushing away the earrings.

'Do you think this is any way to begin Monday morning?' asked a voice from the doorway. Mr le Tissier, our teacher, had arrived.

While Mr le Tissier did the register I had a go at sorting out Dino. Mr le Tissier didn't think much of my idea to put it out for recycling. 'Perhaps it will develop into a further form of evolution, Sir,' I said, but he just snapped at me. Of course, Agnes Potter Higgins offered to help.

'Get lost, Dinosaur's Armpit,' I hissed at her.

'Oh, you are lovely, Wezzie! You're so funny! Dinosaur's Armpit!' She giggled at me. 'He-he-he.'

As I picked up Dino's bits I sank lower and lower into deep despair. Life had little to offer.

Then a small fiend out of Mr Clunthorpe's class came to tell us that we were all to go to the hall, where the headteacher, Mrs Warble, had something important to tell us.

'What have we done now?' asked Kevin gloomily as we made our way there, Agnes Potter H. breathing down my neck.

Ours is a big hall with a platform at one end and doors and steps for doing plays. Mrs Warble stood on the platform. She is a big lady who fills the hall and she has all her hair piled on top and a long multicoloured skirt and long multicoloured legs which look like Joseph's Technicolor dreamcoat. Have you ever thought how boring he must have been telling those dreams all the time? Agnes Potter Higgins does that. Tells her dreams all the time. Other people's dreams can be very boring.

At the sight of Mrs Warble silence fell on us like a smother blanket.

'And we shall all have a lovely day!' cried Mrs Warble after a hymn and a prayer and a few notices, like the netball team losing twenty-four goals to one and the football match being post-poned because of five of the other side being injured and the man at the corner house just down the road from the school complaining about his doorbell being rung and when he answers no one being there. He says it's the school's fault. He blames the children; and the teachers, he

says. Mrs Warble didn't say why we were going to have a lovely day, but just don't any of you ring that bell any more, children. Then she told everyone to sit. When the noise died down and we were sitting, and Mr le Tissier had finished threatening Kevin, we waited. And waited. Mrs

Warble waited. We waited some more. If this keeps up it will be playtime, I thought hopefully.

'Mr Clunthorpe,' called out Mrs Warble to the back of the hall. 'Did you remember the poster?'

'Which poster, Mrs Warble?' he shouted back.

'*The* poster, Mr Clunthorpe.'

'Ah. *That* poster. Kenneth Tebbit, fetch the poster.'

'Wh-wh-wh-which p-p-p-p-poster, sir?'

'The poster on my desk, Tebbit!'

'Y-y-yes, s-s-s-sir,' Kenneth Tebbit stuttered.

There was a noise of someone falling over a body, so we all swivelled round to look. Agnes Potter Higgins blew me a kiss, but I ignored her.

'We shall sing "Lord of the Dance",' cried Mrs Warble.

When Mrs Pooter had found the music, we sang 'Lord of the Dance'. At a signal from Mrs Warble we wandered off into 'doh, a deer, a female deer', followed by 'Strawberry Fields For Ever'. Kevin groaned along beside me. His voice is awful.

At last Kenneth returned, clutching the poster.

'You took a long time, Tebbit,' said Mr Clunthorpe.

'I-it w-w-was s-s-stuffed b-b-behind a c-c-cupboard at the th-the b-back o-of th-the r-room,' Kenneth replied, meaning the poster.

'The caretaker's fault,' said Mr Clunthorpe loudly.

'Children,' cried Mrs Warble, ignoring all this and seizing the the poster. 'Look!'

We looked.

It was a small poster, and the first six or seven rows were near enough to read the words. As the first six or seven rows are the very small Infants, not many of them could read the words anyway.

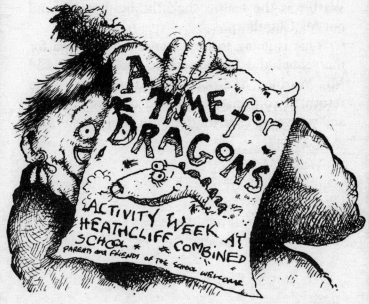

'A Time for Dragons – Activity Week at Heathcliff Combined School. Parents and Friends of the School Welcome,' piped up Penelope, the famous Infant Genius. That's what her mother calls her anyway.

'It's an activity thing,' said Kevin, nudging me.

'Shouldn't affect you much then,' I said.

The noise in the hall grew louder as children threw the words they could read further back down the hall.

Mrs Warble twirled her multicoloured skirt round her multicoloured legs and smiled at us all. The hall fell silent. Perhaps the smile of Mrs Warble is the reason she's the headteacher and not Mr Clunthorpe.

'This is going to be a wonderful occasion for the school and for our whole community,' said Mrs Warble. 'And now, children, I want you to return to your classrooms and discuss *your own* and your class contribution with your teacher.'

**B**ack in the classroom we crowded round Mr le Tissier, who had a copy of the poster. Agnes P. H. squashed up beside me and tried to squeeze my hand. No way. I snatched it back.

'Rotten Gums,' I hissed at her, and shot out of danger behind Kevin. She wouldn't squeeze his hand.

'Quiet, please. Let's look at this poster,' Mr le Tissier said.

'It's not up to much,' Kevin said.

'Well, in that case, we'll all design a poster. A prize for the best one! How about that, children? And since dragons are the theme of our activity week, you can produce something really exciting.'

Mr le Tissier was warming up – his cheeks went pink and he waved his hands about.

I knew Kevin wouldn't know what a theme was, and he didn't.

'What's a theme?' he asked.

Mr le Tissier explained what a theme was and by the time he'd finished nobody knew, let alone Kev. We got ready to do our posters. Or at least, Simon Partington dropped a tin of red powder-paint, which flew everywhere. It took half an hour to sort that out.

'What about maths?' asked Carly.

'Shut up,' everyone hissed at her.

At last we were all settled to create our dragon masterpieces. Maths was now scheduled for *after* play.

'The mayor's opening our Dragon Week. On the Monday afternoon. With the governors and the PTA. I've known all along,' said Carly.

She always knows all along. She's like that.

'Your mother's the mayor,' said Agnes P. H.

'Yes, that's how I've known all along,' smirked Carly.

'Why can't somebody famous open it?' asked Kev. 'Like Kelly Minto.'*

'Oh no, that wouldn't do at all,' shuddered Sir.

'Why can't we have Kelly Minto?' shouted half the class.

'We can't afford her,' sniffed Mr le Tissier.

'We'll have a sponsored something . . .' suggested Simon.

'A crawl,' I said.

'A creep. A sponsored creep would be great,'

* The well-known pop singer.

said Kevin. I thought Mr le Tissier looked as if he might burst.

'This is our school's activity week. We need to show everyone the breadth of this school's horizons and the heights of its achievements. People like Kelly Minto have nothing to do with this. Or anything else . . .' he added.

'We don't mind you hating her, Sir,' Kevin said gently. 'You've got to, really, as you're old and past it.'

'I AM NOT OLD AND PAST IT,' thundered Sir. 'It's just that Kelly Minto is RUBBISH!'

'Oh, Sir.'

'Don't say that, Sir.'

'Don't be like that!'

'She's FANTASTIC!'

'WICKED!'

'BRILL!'

'COSMIC!'

'SUPERSTAR!'

'MEGASTAR!'

'NOT!' bellowed Kev.

'All right, all right, all right. Sit down, children. Shh. Get to your desks. And get off mine! Hush. Hush. Mrs Warble's coming!'

The thought of Mrs Warble coming was enough to make anyone hush, so we sat down and hushed. But, of course, Sir was having us on.

'Sir. About Kelly Minto . . .'

'KEVIN BREWSTER! I don't want to hear that name again. D'you hear me, Kevin?'

'I hear you, Sir. I won't mention Kelly Minto's name again, Sir.'

'She's beautiful,' sighed Carly. 'In my magazine it says she can't choose between her boyfriends.'

'I wish she was my girlfriend,' said Simon.

'BE QUIET!' roared Mr le Tissier.

'Why, Sir?'

'Because you are incapable, absolutely incapable of discussing anything reasonably. All our talks end in chaos.'

'Like the House of Commons, Sir? All of them shouting?'

'Yes. Yes. Yes.'

'We *will* talk sensibly, Sir,' Agnes said.

Mr le Tissier began again.

'I want to tell you about *The Week*. It will be a heavy programme . . .'

'Mind you don't drop it!' put in Kev. Mr le T. ignored him.

'. . . and we shall need to be alert and hard-working. VERY IMPORTANT PEOPLE will be inspecting our work to see what the standards are here, what kind of school it is. So I know you will be on your best behaviour and a credit to the school, Mrs Warble and all of us.'

But I'd stopped listening. I was working on my poster, which was shaping up nicely. My dragon

would definitely be in the top ten. And I'd nearly forgotten all about Agnes Potter Higgins.

In the afternoon Mrs Pooter took us for creative writing. Now this is (secretly) my favourite subject, as I intend to be a writer when I grow up. I *think* about it a lot, but I don't *talk* about it *at all* because in a home and a class like mine it seems a good idea to keep quiet. Still, I do enjoy those lessons where I can write about fantasy and thrills instead of facts and reality. Mr le Tissier was very enthusiastic about my latest story of a prehistoric monster that emerged from a swamp and found its way to a school like ours. But Sir was on a course this afternoon, so it was Mrs Potter, who's the music teacher, taking us. I don't have any musical ambitions and she is *not* my favourite teacher. 'Keep on the note, Wesley. Listen to the note. LISTEN TO THE NOTE, DEAR!'

Agnes had managed to creep in next to me and she copied my idea about a babysitter who turned into a werewolf. The baby was rescued by a brave boy called William. Agnes used the same plot, only her rescuer was a girl called Anna, who was loved, I ask you, by a boy called Walter. The baby's name was Willy – huh.

Mrs Pooter gave an A to her and a C to me. I was mad, crazy, raging. I put out my tongue at her – Agnes, I mean.

'Try to think up ideas of your own,' Mrs Pooter told me. 'Don't copy what others are doing.'

'Thank you very much,' I replied. 'It was my idea in the first place.'

'Agnes is a very original girl.' She smiled gently and widely at me like a frog that's just had a good meal of pond flies – I don't like old Pooter. 'But I'm sure, Wesley dear, that you, too, can manage something if you try hard.'

Spotted slime, rabies and rotten earthworms to you, I answered, but not too loud. Kevin was grinning his head off.

I tried telling Mr le Tissier, who's new and almost young, when he came back at the end of the afternoon.

'Make allowances,' he said. 'Agnes probably has a hard time at home. Instead of moaning, lend a hand.'

'I don't want to lend a hand,' I muttered to Kevin. 'It's like lending a hand to a crocodile stuck in the mud. I'll never get it back.'

Kevin said that he was sick and tired of hearing about Agnes Potter Higgins and would I belt up or go jump in a lake.

'Thank you *very* much,' I said. 'Dog-breath.'

Mr le Tissier separated us and we had to stay in after the others. I tried talking to him – Sir – again. After all, he did say at the beginning of this term that he was here to sort out our problems and don't be afraid to ask. He put down his pen, sighing.

'Wesley, I'm having enough trouble fitting in the Dragon Activity Week with the National Curriculum without trying to sort out Agnes and you as well. Not now. She's a funny girl – like a piece of knotty . . .'

'Nutty or knotty, Sir?'

'Does it matter?' he sighed. 'Right now, Wesley, this desk is full of paperwork I'm not ever going to get through, so if you'll excuse me I'll make a start on not finishing it.' He lowered his voice. 'Oh, by the way, Wesley . . . do they,' he whispered, 'call me Tissue Paper?'

'And worse, Sir.'

'Much worse, Wesley?'

'Much worse, Sir.'

He nodded gloomily.

'Do you want to know, Sir? Would you like to hear what they call you?'

'No, I'm depressed enough as it is, Wesley. You and Kevin can go now.'

Kevin left as fast as he could, not being one to hang around school, but I burbled on.

'Do you like being here with us? Teaching in our school?'

He didn't answer.

'What made you go in for teaching, Sir?'

He put down his pen.

'Haven't you got a home to go to, Wesley?'
'Do you want to go home, Sir?'
He put his head in his hands.
'Well, since you ask me, Wesley . . . Yes. Yes.'

'You've only got to say, Sir.'
'It's just that I've got a lot of work . . . Good-bye, Wesley.'
'You're sure you don't need me for anything?'
'I – don't – need – you – for – anything – Wesley.'
'It's just – just that she waits for me, Sir. Her. Agnes.'

'Oh. I see. I think she'll be gone by now. You should be safe, Wesley.'

I slithered out of school like a silent snake through the sinister woods. Kev had left ages ago.

The road home was empty, hardly any kids about. I turned into my street, no sign of Agnes. I started to whistle. Then I stopped whistling.

She'd shot out from an alleyway, holding a frozen chocolate bar.

Now, I'm only human, so I took it, muttering thanks.

Her smile was so wide the corners got lost in her earrings. Agnes Potter Higgins was pleased. I licked the scrumptious frozen bar and tried not to see her, moving as fast as I could, but she kept up with me, trotting like a pony.

'Can I come home with you, Wezzie? I've never been in your home, Wezzie. Not all the time I've known you. Please, Wezzie.'

I almost dropped the chocolate. My stomach dropped as well. What a terrible moment. Was there nowhere safe? I bit the frozen end too quickly and it slid ever so slowly, slowly, slowly down my throat . . .

'Please. It's horrible at my house with all those girls. I don't like them much. I'd rather go home with you. Please, Wezzie.'

I couldn't speak. My throat was in Antarctica. I'd got to swallow it quickly, as we don't have chocolate at home. I couldn't say no. And that was how she got inside our house.

# Chapter Three

Mum had carrot juice and her special energy beanies – her own recipe – waiting for us. My dad and two older brothers, Rock and Cliff, had arrived already, all keen and raring to go. Dad starts work very early in the morning so he can be home in time to train and bodybuild all three of us Baker boys. It's worked with them. Cliff's over six foot and he's the *little* one. They're both in the school basketball team – they call Rock 'Wonder Bake' and Cliff 'Special Bake'. They play rugger as well, and table tennis and everything. My mum is a black belt first dan in aikido and held her school's record for the long jump. Still does, I think. But none of this works with me. I'm still little, thin and weedy. I don't put my heart into things, Dad shouts. His voice is twice as loud as any normal person's. And he's right, I don't.

'You've got to have heart. Miles and miles of

heart,' he sings at the top of his enormous voice. Sometimes he looks at me and his eyes – very big eyes, everything about Dad is supersized – fill with tears.

'I don't believe it,' he sighs. 'I just don't believe it. It's not possible. But I'll make a man of him yet, I promise, O Lord, I promise.' And he shakes his huge fists in the air.

But I don't. Grow, I mean. I stay me.

'Perhaps we should stretch him,' grins Rock.

'The rack,' laughs Cliff.

'He'd be skinnier than ever!' And they fall about, ha ha.

Dad says I've got to laugh as well, as I've got to learn to TAKE A JOKE! You can go off JOKES if they're always on you.

Agnes beamed at everybody. She swigged down carrot juice (how I hate carrot juice).

'Great,' she gulped, ate about twenty energy beanies and asked for another carrot juice.

'Hello,' she said at last.

'Hello,' said my dad. 'Going to join us for a session?'

'Yeah. Oh, please.'

'Well, you haven't got the right kit.'

'I'll find you something,' said my mum, 'while Wesley gets changed.'

Agnes came back looking crazy in a very old

leotard and a woolly hat so there was no need for her to fall about laughing at me in my kit.

'Shut up,' I muttered, as she pointed at me.

'I can't help it. It's – you're – such a funny shape. Oh, I do love you, Wezzie.'

'SHUT UP,' I screamed. But too late. Cliff and Rock had heard . . .

'She loves him,' sang Cliff.

'Yeah, yeah, yeah!' sang Rock. They held one another, weeping.

I'm not often grateful to my dad, but, 'Enough!' he roared. 'Let's get going! Time for warm-ups and the programme!'

Dad's transformed our shed into a home gymnasium. And if you think our house is spotless and full of gadgets (and it is), then you should see Dad's pride and joy, the gymnasium. In it he's got a multi-gym and butterfly unit on which you can learn every skill you ever wanted (or didn't want). Then there's an exercise bicycle, a bullworker, a chest expander, benches for sitting up, folding up, curling legs, a punchball, a rowing machine, a treadmill and loads of other things.

'Oh, isn't it absolutely fabulously beautiful,' cried Agnes, rushing to the multi-gym and hugging it. 'I've never seen one before.'

They all showed her round proudly.

Dance music reverberated throughout the shed and we began: bouncing, hopping, skipping, stretching, jumping, star-jumping, leaping, running round the outside of the gym, then cartwheels, somersaults . . .

Dad often records us with his camcorder and we all get a good laugh at the sight of me warming up with my brothers. There's a shot of me standing on Rock's shoulders, and one of Cliff holding me upside down with one hand. Of the two of them I'd rather have Rock, he's not quite so, well, so . . .

'Press-ups now,' bellowed Dad. 'Up and down, thrust and push, keep on going, don't give in, break your record, stretch and strain, grunt and groan, BREATHE DEEPLY NOW!'

After a bit I lay down on a mat and thought about dying, not caring much if I did.

But the others kept going. Even Agnes. Especially Agnes!

'Thirty-eight, thirty-nine, forty,' she counted, cheeks glowing.

'Hey, the kid's good,' cried Rock, pausing to watch.

'Not bad for a girl,' said Cliff.

They were all beaming at her.

'Better than Wesley,' said Rock.

'That's not difficult,' cried Cliff.

They next moved in turn on to the multi-gym, working arms and legs and chests.

'Come on, Wesley,' shouted Dad.

'Come on, Wezzie,' shouted Agnes, going forward and back, up and down.

I pretended to push the pads, hoping Dad wouldn't concentrate on me because he was busy demonstrating to Agnes. She was well away.

'What a lovely girl!' cried my mother, coming in. She does her workout earlier in the day. 'What a find! Why didn't you bring her home before, Wesley?'

I gave up pretending to try, and sat on the mat. Words failed me, though the idea for a story about the end of the world suddenly jumped into my brain.

'Stay for tea, my dear,' invited my mother after another half an hour's torture. (Dad had made me join in again.)

'I'd love to,' said Agnes. 'I like your house so much. It's so clean and organized. I'd love some proper sports kit like yours.'

'Ask your mother to get some for you.'

'Oh, all our stuff comes from jumble sales, and Mum puts it in a chest and we fish out what we can. Tryphena always gets the best as she's the biggest,' Agnes said. 'And the horriblest,' she added. 'Sophie wore my clothes yesterday.'

'Extraordinary!' said my mum.

'What a wonderful spread,' beamed Agnes later, patting her stomach. She'd just eaten steak, mushrooms, beans, green salad, bangers, a fresh fruit salad and half a loaf. I couldn't manage mine. All

our food is for BODYBUILDING. I'd love some jelly or something like that, sometimes; just now and then.

'Get it all down you!' roared Dad. 'Look at your friend here! Fine girl.'

I looked the other way after I saw Agnes had got food on her earrings and down her front.

'You'll never grow big and strong like the rest of us,' bellowed Dad.

'But I don't want to be like the rest of you!' I muttered.

'Oh, you are funny,' cried Agnes.

'She loves you, Wezzie,' sang Rock.

'Yeah, yeah, yeah,' followed up Cliff.

I stood up.

'You might be big, you lot, but you're all STUPID! I don't want to be like you – robot bodybuilders. I'd rather be – an – an EGG-HEAD!'

They were still laughing as I rushed upstairs and wedged my bedroom door tight shut. But they soon got me out, and back doing exercises.

Much later, after Agnes had gone at last, escorted safely home by Rock and Cliff, I crept out of my bedroom window on to the garage roof, down behind the garden bushes and round the back of the shed where there's a hole through to Kev's garden, which backs on to ours; a secret path. Dad doesn't think much of Kev and his family.

Once inside, Peachey, Kev's sister, gave me a hot squelchy cream doughnut. She's beautiful, Kev's sister, though she eats all the things my dad says are poison. All the things I like. She doesn't laugh at me either. I think I nearly love Peachey, but she's seventeen, a bit old for me. The Brewsters all do restful things like watching telly or reading or playing cards or doing crosswords. Mr Brewster had a can of beer beside him.

The Brewster home is comfy and relaxed and I don't have to be something I'm not when I'm there. They've got big old armchairs and sofas with comics and magazines and paperbacks stuffed down the sides, and a hairy dog called Baggins, who lies on you and licks you when you're miserable. If you want to go off in a room by yourself to build a tower or write a story or play with computer games you can. Nobody takes any notice. My dad won't let me touch our computer unless he's with me organizing it all. The Brewsters don't have menus and timetables and noticeboards full of PTA and church meetings and dentist's appointments in their kitchen. Best of all, you can do *nothing* there, with nobody disturbing you. All my best ideas come when I look as if I'm doing nothing. My dad hates people doing nothing. 'Idle hands mischief find,' he says.

'Come upstairs,' Kevin said. He'd got a fantastic beetle in a matchbox, big and green and shiny. We thought up names for it. Napoleon, we ended up with, then we let it go in the garden and carried on with the tree-house we're always building in the old apple tree, but we can't get it to balance. My dad would have fixed it properly, whereas *we* like fiddling about with it. Baggins helped.

'Agnes Potter . . . ' I began.

'Shut up,' said Kevin. So I did.

## Chapter Four

School went crazy. Well, it always is, but I mean worse than usual.

Posters . . . murals . . . stories . . . pictures . . . models . . . jokes . . . poems . . . songs . . . plays . . .

'Dragons here, dragons there, dragons, dragons everywhere!' sang A.P.H., short for Agnes Potter Higgins of course.

'Our Dragon Week is a Quest for Knowledge,' Mrs Warble told us in assembly. 'Afterwards we shall all be wiser and better.'

Her hair fell in a waterfall down her back and she shimmered blue and silver, like a mermaid, said A.P.H.

Everywhere a space could be found, children could also be found working – bodies in corners, corridors, cloakrooms, outdoors, indoors, canteen and hall.

'*We* shan't waste time,' Mr Clunthorpe told his class. '*We* shall stick to the curriculum, paying special attention to maths and spelling.'

'He's a hard man,' his class told the rest of us at lunchtime. 'We wrote out spellings ALL MORNING.'

Soon poems and stories about dragons hung on the walls: little dragons, big dragons, green dragons, red dragons, gold dragons, baby dragons, Welsh dragons, Chinese dragons, dragons of myth and dragons of history.

Books about dragons appeared all over the school. Some very old ones were brought out and dusted off.

The school orchestra began to rehearse the 'Dragon' Symphony, written by Mrs Pooter. She tested everyone for their ability in either singing or playing an instrument, and rejected Kev and me immediately. Agnes she dithered over – but Sophie landed the solo part of Amazonia, the Warrior Maiden.

We had one of our classroom chats with Mr le Tissier as he was writing his version of *St George and the Dragon*, to be performed on the last afternoon of Dragon Week. I knew I could have done it better, but he didn't accept my offer.

'Mrs Warble talked of Quests,' he told us, arms waving and nearly knocking over Carly's flower arrangement. 'This is a kind of Quest, too. A Quest for Perfection.'

Kev pinged Simon Partington with a rubber band just then and there was a scuffle.

'Where was I?' asked Mr le Tissier. 'Oh yes. A Quest for Perfection. This we shall try to achieve in our performance. Now, I've written the play and we'll try out the actors I've selected. Agnes, you shall be the captive princess.'

'Why not me?' cried Carly. 'I'm much quicker at learning lines and I'm prettier.'

'No, you aren't,' cried Kev. 'You look like the back of a bus that's got smashed in. Doesn't she, Wez?'

I didn't answer, or it might have meant I thought Agnes was pretty.

Tim Waring said, 'They're both 'orrible, but Carly is more 'orrible. Always was, Carly. Dead ugly.'

Carly rose in her seat, face purple.

When all was quiet again Mr le Tissier said, 'That's settled then. Agnes is the princess. Simon Partington can have a try at St George, and Kevin will make a wonderful dragon.'

'No way. Drag off,' he yelled, and ran, but was fetched back to have a long talk alone with Mrs Warble.

'I'm the dragon,' he said, when he came back

37

to the classroom.

'What did she say to you,' I asked him later, 'on your long talk?'

'She said, "You're the dragon, Kevin," and I said, "Yes, Mrs Warble."'

'Just like that?'

'Just like that.'

'And Agnes Potter Higgins is going to be the princess.' I fell about laughing; it was hilarious.

'Shut up,' he answered. 'I know. BELT UP!'

'I can't help it. I think it's brill. It's hard to stop laughing!'

But I stopped very easily the next day, when Mr le Tissier called me up to his desk.

'Wesley, I'd like a word.'

'Yes, Mr le Tissier.' I felt no alarm, no warning inside of trouble ahead.

'You see, Mrs Partington has phoned us to say that Simon broke his ankle at the Woodcraft folk class last night and she doesn't think he'll be able to play St George.'

'Oh, bad luck,' I said sympathetically. 'Poor old Simon.' (I can't stand him.)

'Well, we'd like *you* to play St George instead. Mrs Warble thinks you will be wonderful in the part and, of course, you get on so well with Agnes it should all work out nicely.'

'SIR! Sir, I'm no good at acting! Besides, you want someone strong. I'm not the hero type.'

'You underestimate yourself, Wesley.'

'But, but, I can't stand Agnes Potter Higgins. I hate Agnes Potter Higgins. I don't want to rescue her from a dragon. I'd like – I'd like the

dragon to eat Agnes Potter Higgins! I told you, Mr le Tissier, I told you how I felt about her! How can you do this to me, Sir? In front of the whole school. And the Mayor. And the Governors. I can't bear it.'

'I think you'd better go and have a long talk with Mrs Warble, Wesley.'

I stood in front of Mrs Warble's desk in her room. Maybe it was the sun shining through the window, but she shimmered, blue and pink and gold and silver.

'You'll be St George, Wesley, won't you?' she said gently.

'Yes, Mrs Warble.'

'And slay the dragon.'

'Yes, Mrs Warble.'

'And rescue the maiden. Dear Agnes.'

'Yes, Mrs Warble.'

'That's settled, then. Good boy. You can do anything you want. Always remember that, Wesley.'

I tried to remember her words back at home. Dad told me that he'd written to Mrs Warble and the Governors to complain that the Dragon Week programme, which had been sent out to all the parents, was quite inadequate. There *must* be a sports day.

'I intend to donate a cup, and I expect you to win it, my boy! Don't stand there with your mouth hanging open – we're going to start a whole new programme, now! A WESLEY THE WINNER programme!'

## Chapter Five

'No, Wesley, not like that! You must put real feeling into it! You have slain the dragon, the onlookers are shouting your name, this is your moment of triumph, as you break the chains that bind the captive princess to the rock outside the dragon's cave and you take her hand and draw her towards you, Wesley . . .'

Mr le Tissier's face shone, his arms waved, his eyes sparkled, his hair stood on end. Mr le Tissier was happy. Mr le Tissier was inspired. Mr le Tissier loved drama. 'Think of it as a Quest, Wesley,' he cried.

Why doesn't *he* do it, then, since he feels so strongly about it, I thought bitterly.

'Wezzie. Just remember I love you. Take my hand, Wezzie. You are my hero. You are my knight in shining white armour. Wezzie, I'm your princess,' murmured Agnes, stretching out her arms, which I managed to dodge.

Kevin, the dragon, lying captured at my feet, was grinning his head off and murmuring, 'I love you too, Wezzie,' softly so that no one could hear but me. I stamped my foot down hard on his defeated stomach and prodded him with the stick I was using as a sword. He stopped saying I love you, Wezzie, and shouted, 'Ouch,' instead.

'Good, that's very good, Kevin,' cried Mr le Tissier. 'You're a natural, I think.'

He paced up and down. He'd really taken to this playwriting stuff. He was growing his hair and designer stubble, and wearing an antique dark red velvet jacket and a black flowing tie. Mr Clunthrope was heard muttering and complaining that the next thing would be teachers wandering around in T-shirts and Bermuda shorts, that's what the school was coming to.

Anyway, Mr le Tissier turned to the onlookers (the countryside scourge and so on), who had followed St George to the dragon's cave in the hope of seeing him devoured by the evil beast, and showed them how to let themselves go, and get into the spirit of their roles. Tim Waring did some monkey jumps and Tarzan warblings. I prodded Kevin again as it made me feel better. Under cover of Sir directing the rabble, Agnes was murmuring.

'Wezzie, come home with me, Wezzie.'

'No!'

Mr le Tissier said, 'Now, let's have one more go at releasing the captive princess, Wesley.'

'Oh no, Sir,' I sighed. Into my mind floated a vision of a huge, red, green and gold dragon. As I watched, fascinated, he unfurled his vast wings and rippled the coils of an enormous tail. I blinked and he'd gone.

'What's the matter, Wesley?'

'I'm tired, Sir.'

'Did you go to bed late?'

'No, it's not that.'

'What is it then?'

'Nothing.'

I couldn't bring myself to tell him that Dad had had me practising the one hundred metres, the hundred-metre hurdles, the long jump and the high jump for hours the night before.

'You're going to win a cup if it kills me, Wesley,' he said.

'It's not you it'll kill, it'll be me,' I muttered under my breath.

'All our family have been athletes. I was Victor Ludorum of my school. Your Uncle Fred was the area cross-country champion. Your Aunt Davina won the county hurdles. Your grandfather played cricket for a minor county, I know, but he holds the record number of runs.'

'Don't go on, Dad. I don't care, anyway.'

'Nonsense, me lad. You've just got to persevere, that's all. Look at your brothers . . .'

'Please, Dad, no. I can't bear looking at my brothers. They make me feel ill . . .'

In the end he had to let me go, and in the end Mr le Tissier let us go because he'd looked at the hall clock and seen that it was later than he'd thought.

Back we went to the classroom, where we had to complete a whole load of maths to put on the wall display units and write out a dragon poem in our very best script, also for display. Wearily I reached out for a book, any old book would do.

'Sir?' I yawned.

'Yes, Wesley?'

'Is "The Lambton Worm" a kind of dragon, Sir?'

'Yes, it is, Wesley. Yes, you may use that one.'

## THE LAMBTON WORM

Whisht lads, haud your gobs
I'll tell ye all an awful story
Whisht lads, haud your gobs
I'll tell ye 'boot the worm.

Now this worm got fat and growed
                  and growed
And growed an awful size
Wi' greet big head and greet big gob
And great big goggly eyes
And when, at neets, he crawled about
To pick up bits of news
If he felt dry upon the road
He milked a dozen coos.

What was I doing writing out this dreadful poem? 'Rock-a-bye, baby, on the tree-top' was more in my line, I was so knackered. If I wasn't

46

so tired I'd write my own. It must be nearly home-time. Oh no, not that programme again. Oh . . . dear . . . no . . . Please, please, no.

I seemed to hear Dad saying, 'Just a thousand more press-ups, Wesley. Come on now. No shirking, or the dragon will get you.'

He smiled at me and the smile changed into the smile of the dragon looking straight at me, wreaths of smoke blowing all over me, covering me, till I couldn't see anything at all.

I came to to find Mr le Tissier shaking me.

'Wesley, wake up, Wesley . . . It's time to go home.'

And at the gate, who should be waiting but Agnes. I turned to flee, but I couldn't outrun Agnes. She grabbed me; her sisters joined her, and that's how I found myself in the awful car with the nodding dogs, the girls holding me down.

# Chapter Six

I once read a story called 'A Living Nightmare', and now I was caught in one myself. The Horror Story of the Year – worse than the most scary horror film; worse than running the hundred metres for the third time; worse than fifty press-ups; worse than a hundred hurdles, this was IT, the end, the pits, the ULTIMATE DOOM.

Worn out, knackered, with sports practice the previous evening, tests during the morning and rehearsing *St George and the Dragon* in the afternoon, I'd been caught off guard and had let myself be seized and TRAPPED.

Which is how I came to be in the Potter Higgins' home with Agnes, while all around us sounded the noise of the Potter Higgins girls practising the music composed by Mrs Pooter for the 'Dragon' Symphony.

Mrs Potter Higgins was holding out her hands

(and about fifty bracelets on her wrists) to me. Greying hair in ringlets fell to her waist and she wore purple velvet trousers.

'My dear, do you have an instrument?' I jumped. She had a really deep voice.

'The recorder,' I muttered. 'I can just about play the recorder. At school.'

'Then I shall give you some lessons myself. You simply *must* have an instrument. Mustn't he, Agnes, dear?' She bent over me and ringlets dangled all around. 'Agnes has the oboe.'

'Oh, I'm sorry,' I stammered. 'I didn't know. Does it hurt?'

Agnes kicked me, so I shut up. Mrs Potter Higgins pressed my hand.

'William – now, is your name William?'

'It's Wesley, Mum. I told you.'

'Of course. I remember. Dear Agnes. Always call me Cecilia, dear, not Mum. Of course, Wellsley, I must tell you that Agnes doesn't possess darling Sophie's phenomenal gifts or Melody's perfect pitch or Tryphena's extraordinary virtuosity, but there – she'll improve with practice, determination and perseverance, won't you, darling?'

I couldn't follow all this, but I know about practice, don't I just?

'If Agnes has got to do her practice now, I'll go home,' I said hopefully. 'I wouldn't want to stop Agnes doing her practice – honest.'

'Nonsense, dear boy. William, it is William, isn't it?'

'No; Wesley,' said Agnes grimly. 'I told you.'

'Yes, of course you did, dear. Wellsley, I'll find you a recorder. We've lots of spares. Then I'll get all the girls together and we'll make jolly, jolly music, won't we, Agnes, darling? Girls, girls, Sophie, Melody, Tryphena, come, come, musical fun-times! With darling William here! Agnes's little friend. Come along, girls.'

'Mum, I just wanted to show him the garden and the pond . . .' said Agnes.

'Ah, there you all are, girls. Aren't *all* my darling, precious angels lovely, Wellsley? Tryphena, just fetch William a recorder. What shall we start with?'

'Let's try the Beethoven,' said Sophie.

'No, the Chopin,' put in Melody.

'It'll have to be something easy for him,' sneered Tryphena, handing me a recorder. 'He looks stupid. What about "Three Blind Mice"?'

'That's it,' cried her mother. "Now then, all together . . . Are we ready? One, Two, Three Blind Mice . . .'

I lifted the recorder and blew. Nothing happened. I blew again and made a noise so rude I nearly dropped the instrument. My face flashed up like a beacon right to the tips of my ears.

I'm sorry if I've been a bad boy, I prayed inwardly. But save me now. Please. I'll be good

for ever and I'll try to win a race for Dad and I'll
try to be a good St George. But get me out of
here! Oh, please!

'Which of you has had my dictionary?' boomed
a voice from the doorway. A bald-headed man
with a long black and grey tangled beard and
'tache, looking like Moses or somebody out of
the Bible, stood there, dressed in a shirt thing, a
bit like a maternity smock – I know about them
as Kev's mum's wearing one right now – and
brown plastic sandals revealing dirty feet with
long toenails.

My prayers have been answered, I thought,
nearly falling on my knees as Mrs P.H. stopped
conducting. I put down the recorder.

'I'll get your dictionary, Theophilus, dear. It's
in the upstairs loo, where I was looking something up when the phone went and I had to
dash.'

'Haven't you got your own?' asked Theophilus
dear. 'People are always taking mine!'

I closed my eyes and prayed again. The music
had staggered to a halt, but I still wanted to get
away from this madhouse. No wonder A.P.H.
was barmy. Actually, she didn't seem so bad
amongst all the rest of them.

'Girls,' trilled Mrs P.H., or Cecilia, as she
liked to be called, 'let's find the dictionary and
then we'll all get tea together for dear Wellsley
here, and the rest of us, of course. Theophilus,

dear – you just retire to your study and get on with your lovely wonderful writing and we'll call you when we're ready.'

Theophilus dear disappeared, falling over a pile of books as he went, for there were dozens of them everywhere; books here, books there, books and leaflets everywhere. I'd never seen so many books anywhere outside a library. I wanted to read all of them from cover to cover. Agnes's home had books and music like mine had sports and keep-fit equipment.

'Come *on*, Wesley, we've got to find eggs for tea,' shouted Melody – at least, I think it was Melody, as Tryphena was the one who kept pulling horrible faces at me, and Sophie, the gifted wonder, looked as if she wasn't on this planet.

'Don't forget some leaves!' cried Mrs P.H. 'We must have leaves for tea.'

My heart, already sinking fast, fell even lower. Why were we finding eggs? Didn't they just have them in the kitchen, like us?

Our kitchen is so full of white, bright, shining, antiseptic equipment it looks like an anti-germ lab. Somehow I didn't think the Potter Higgins' kitchen would be like that, and it wasn't. I could see as we made our way through it – a dark obstacle course full of old pots, cats, mouldy bread, feathery leaves, more cats, decaying onions and heaps of washing. Several really interesting

53

toadstools or mushrooms flourished on the walls – in fact it was just like living inside a giant, hollowed-out fungus. The cat sitting on the butter on the draining-board swiped angrily at me as I went past.

'I haven't done anything,' I hissed back at it.

But at least I didn't have to worry about dirty

footprints like I do at home. Clean ones would be the problem here.

'C'mon, Wezzie, I do so want to show you the garden,' said Agnes, and grabbed my hand. I snatched it away, but I felt a bit sorry for her. She didn't seem to be as awful here as at school; at least she wasn't as bad as her revolting sisters. Into the garden we went.

Have you see those pictures of countries suffering from pollution and worse? Agnes's garden looked like that. A few animals and hens wandered about among the weeds.

'We're organically pure!' cried Mrs P.H. from behind me. 'So wonderful. Come and see my herbs, William!'

She seized my hand – yuk – and together we

squelched to a six-foot-high splodge of stinging-nettles in the far corner.

'I just adore nettle soup,' she shrilled. 'Don't you, Wellsley?'

'I've – I've – never had any . . .'

'You haven't? Then you must come to supper. Soon. Now, that's a date, Wellsley! I know you're Agnes's friend, but you shall be mine as well! I never had a dear little boy.'

I tried to pull my hand away and to move my feet, but she held on tight, and so did the mud to my feet. Mum was going to do her nut about this later.

'I've got one,' shrieked Tryphena. 'I've got an egg.'

'I didn't know goats laid eggs!' I cried, for the awful Tryphena was surrounded by three bearded animals.

'Oh, you are funny, Wezzie!' shrieked Agnes, joining us. 'I've got another egg. That's two.'

'Oh, goody,' said her mum. 'Wellsley, you do love fresh eggs and beautiful home-baked bread, don't you?'

'Yes, I think so. That egg's very dirty, Agnes,' I said, and waited to hear 'You're so funny, Wezzie!' but she sighed instead.

'Yeah, I know. I always have to wash 'em and the sink's full of filthy dishes.' She sounded down, for Agnes.

'Oh, silly girl!' cried Mum P.H. (or Mumpy H.). 'You should be glad to do little things for our lovely, lovely family.'

'What about Sophie? She gets out of everything.'

'Oh, but Sophie's so gifted. We must make allowances.'

'And the other two? Why does it always have to be ME? Or are they gifted as well?'

'Well – darling – you know we all love you. You're our special person. Our rock on which we build, create; from which we fly!'

Agnes sighed heavily. I think she'd heard it all before.

I managed to get my feet out of the mud and my hand away from Mumpy H. then I took a

few steps forward and found myself ankle-deep in oozy squelch.

'The pond!' cried Agnes. 'My pond. All the water's gone again . . .'

'Not all of it! There's plenty of water where I'm standing!' I said.

'It keeps draining away! I fill it up and then it goes. Oh, here's a dead fish. And another. And another. That's little Freddie. Oh, oh, oh!'

Agnes wailed, the girls crowded round. I thought perhaps I could creep off home while they were all busy weeping and carrying-on over the fish. I headed furtively towards the house, the kitchen, the hall, the front door and home.

But it was no good.

'Where are you going?' shouted Tryphena, grabbing me. 'Rushing off. Pig.'

'C'mon,' said Agnes. 'Come and have some . . . tea . . . I had a lovely meal at your house.' Her voice was wistful. 'But don't expect food like that here.'

I was glad Agnes had warned me. The eggs were boiled so hard you could have left the shells on and not noticed any difference. The lettuce leaves and watercress came complete with caterpillars and beetles, and the bread . . .

'Don't try to eat it,' hissed Agnes. 'It'll break your teeth. Just drop it under the table.'

Rock-cakes followed. They had the right name.

I had to eat them, though.

At last I got home. Mum and Dad went on for ages about the mud I'd brought in and because I'd missed the programme and was late for tea. I tried to eat the enormous meal kept for me, but I fell asleep beside the plate and dreamt about the dragon again. He was coiled, sleeping, around a house. I tiptoed towards him, but he didn't wake, so I slipped between his coils and peered in at the window. I was looking at piles of books everywhere, hundreds of them; old leather books with gold lettering on the spines. I peered hard, straining my eyes to see properly and read *My Adventure* by Wesley Randolph Baker. This made me very happy and I tried to get in at the window, but the coils round me began to move and the books changed to dead fish and hard-boiled eggs. Smoke billowed over the house and I woke up sweating as hard as if I'd been doing my programme.

# Chapter Seven

'Leave me alone. I don't want to win the hundred metres or anything else! I don't want to be St George killing dragons. I've got nothing against dragons. They never did anything to me. I don't want my dad and Agnes P.H. chasing me all the time. I just want to do my own thing and be left in peace. Let me be me!'

'What are you muttering to yourself for?' Kevin shouted in my ear, jolting me awake. 'You gone nutty or somethin'? More nutty than usual, I mean?'

Everybody lifted up their heads, including Agnes. It was afternoon and we were drawing maps for a classroom atlas. Mr le Tissier was on a stepladder, wrestling with yet another dragon on the far side of the room. I'd managed to get a place a fair way away from Agnes, with Kevin between as a barricade. But she kept negotiating with sir and other people to close in on me.

'You must be off your rocker fancying that knobbly-kneed, jug-eared nit,' said Tim Waring.

'But that's why,' cried Agnes. 'That's why I love him, because of his knees and his jug-ears. They're lovely.'

The class roared, naturally, but I sat silent. I'd heard it all before and I was bored, bored out of my tiny mind.

The evening before, she'd joined us on the council sports field and beaten me at everything.

'Come on, Potty Higgins,' my brothers were shouting at one point. She didn't seem to mind. She was brilliant. Dad clapped her on the back and told her she was a great girl.

When the agony was over I rushed up to bed, but then, fed up, I crept out through the window, over the garage and through the secret exit to Kevin's.

Peachey had made pancakes, and smiled at me.

'Children, children,' called out Mr le Tissier, perched on top of the stepladder, which wobbled perilously.

'Look out, Sir, I'll help you,' shouted Agnes, and rushed forward. The stepladder swayed, then suddenly its legs shot outwards, and opened out flat on the floor, with Mr le Tissier seated on the rungs.

'Oh dear, oh dear, oh dear,' he wailed, rubbing himself.

One half of the class cried, 'Oh, Sir.' ... 'Are you all right, Sir?' ... 'Poor Sir.' ... 'Never mind!' ... 'Let me help.' ... 'Poor Mr le Tissier.'

The other half were going, 'Ho-ho-ho! Ha-ha-ha! Tee-hee-hee!'

Lots of kids rushed forward to help him, but not me. I was still too knackered. He tried to get up, but was encumbered by the mobile on his head, the stepladder under his feet and ten or so kids helping him to rise.

Into this whirlpool of activity swanned Mrs Warble, multicoloured skirts swirling.

'Oh, we are busy,' she smiled. 'Such a happy class this one. Where's Mr le Tissier?'

'There,' pointed two dozen fingers.

'Here,' squeaked a voice. And Mr le Tissier emerged from the mini-scrum, still wearing the dragon mobile. Silence fell on us all.

Mrs Warble smiled and removed the mobile. Children slid back to their seats, except for me. I hadn't moved.

'How is the play progressing? I'm so looking forward to it. I'm sure it will be a wholly wonderful, worthwhile experience.'

'Oh, it's coming along well.' Mr le Tissier

63

squeaked a bit. He looked as if something was hurting.

'It's a madhouse here,' I muttered to Simon P., now back at school, his broken ankle in plaster with all our names on it.

'You've nothing to complain about,' he hissed at me. 'Agnes gives you sweets every day. And you haven't got a broken ankle and a broken home. My dad's gone off again.'

Feeling guilty, I pushed the latest Agnes offering – a box of chocs – on to his desk.

Limping awkwardly, Mr le Tissier had reached *his* desk and sat down, rather pale, then he stood up again, wincing.

'I need volunteers to tidy the room and then I want you all to be very quiet and peaceful, please. Get out your reading books and we'll have a silent half-hour while I sort things out.'

I settled with a book, but in no time at all the dragon flew in front of my page with huge, beautiful swoops and swirls. I was no longer in the classroom, but on the top of a high cliff that overlooked not the sea, but a deep wooded valley. I felt as if I'd always known this strange landscape and the winged monster that seemed to rule over it all. He swooped down into the valley, and I knew that was his lair, his secret place. A very bright sun shone from a painted sky and then the dragon's wings flew across it and everything went dark.

An elbow dug into my ribs.

'You're snoring,' hissed Kevin in my ear. 'You potty or somethin'! Always zizzing, you are.'

'It's time to clear up, children,' called out Mr le Tissier.

I tidied up a bit for him after school.

'You'd better hurry, Wesley. There's a staff meeting. And a curriculum course after that.'

'You work hard, Sir,' I said, as I picked up a very old rabbit's foot from under Kev's desk and put it in my pocket. Baggins would like it, I thought. I must sneak out to see him tonight.

'I never quite catch up with it all,' Mr le T. went on. His drama glow had gone today and he was wearing his old chalky. He looked like a giant panda with black rings round his eyes.

'You *don't* look very well, Sir.'

'I can tell *you*, Wesley, teaching's a bit of a strain. My mother worries about me. Did you know I thought of applying to the police force? Better pay, fewer children.'

'You wouldn't cope, Sir.'

'I suppose not. But I'm not coping anyway.'

'Oh, you are, Sir, you are. We all like you very much.'

'You're a nice boy, Wesley.'

'Then I wish you wouldn't make me play St George, Sir. That's what I really wanted to talk about.'

He shook his head wearily.

'It's Mrs Warble. She sees you as St George. Understand?'

'Yes, Sir.'

'Well, I must go. Some of the other teachers are very keen.'

'So's my dad. D'you know him?'

Mr le Tissier shuddered, but stopped himself quickly.

'Oh, yes. Comes to all the PTA meetings.'

'Yes.'

'He thinks the PE, games and athletics standard isn't high enough, Wesley. We're to have a new, improved sports day.'

'I know.'

'He's offered a cup and special coaching.'

'Yes, Sir.'

'Very kind of your dad, Wesley.'

'Yes, Sir.'

Mrs Pooter stood in the doorway.

'We're all waiting for you in the staff-room, Mr le Tissier.'

'Oh, I'm coming, I'm coming, sorry, sorry,' said Mr le Tissier, limping after her.

'What are you doing here, Wesley? Time you went home instead of hanging about here making a mess. Get along with you,' Mrs Pooter said.

I crept round to the back gate, but it was no good. She was there.

'Like my new earrings, Wezzie?'

'No. Look, I'm going to watch Kevin at the football practice.'

'I'll come with you.'

'Then I won't bother, Agnes Potty Higgins. Stop hanging about for me. I want to go home on my *own*. *See?*'

Peals of laughter echoed up to the sky, making me jump.

'Oh, you are funny, Wezzie. Come on.'

I came on. *What else could I do?*

# Chapter Eight

Agnes's father was in the hall when she got me to her house.

'Come in here, boy,' he said. 'Come and talk to me.' He led me into a room, its walls lined with books. The smell was very ripe in here. I wasn't sure whether it was the four cats, Theophilus dear's feet, the mouldering books or the plate of old food in the grate.

'Sit down,' he said.

I couldn't find anywhere to sit as every chair was piled high. In the end I shifted a violin, a soup plate and a pile of old towels off one and plonked myself down. He burbled away to me as if he'd known me all his life and we were a couple of old mates. He didn't seem too awful. But fancy him being a dad. Funny shapes, sizes and ages dads come in.

'You know about my work, don't you? Well, my life's work on the shift of vowel sounds from the Mediterranean and Scandinavia through Eastern Europe into Siberia and Mongolia has reached an impasse, a hiatus. I mean my work has come to an end. You follow me, boy?'

'Yes,' I muttered, meaning no. I hadn't a clue what he was talking about.

'I really need to gain experience in the field . . .'

'Wouldn't your garden do, sir?' I asked, anxious to be helpful.

'No, no, no, boy. You're not following me. I really need to travel across Europe and Asia and converse at grass-roots level. You follow me?'

'Yes, oh yes, sir. The field.' It had got to be the field. Agnes's dad wanted to buy a field. I didn't know why, but why not? If it made him happy . . .

'Yes, good boy. You comprehend. Unfortunately, I need money.'

I nodded. 'My dad's always on about money.'

'And there's no money in the Potter Higgins' house. Not with all those girls wanting things.'

'My dad always wants to buy new training equipment. And it's expensive. So I understand your problems, sir.'

'Those girls always need another musical instrument.'

'Don't think about them, sir. I try not to.'

'Unfortunately, I have to. Cecilia insists. And you see, boy, I don't seem able to get a grant.

When I get to an interview they don't really want to know me. I wish I knew what was wrong.'

It's the feet, I thought, but I said, 'I'll ask my dad. He's good at sorting things out. And I think you'd go down well in Mongolia. And Siberia. The smock, y'know, Mr Potter Higgins. It'd fit there.'

'Doctor. Doctor Potter Higgins.'

'Oh, I didn't know you were one of *them*. Measles and operations.'

'I'm not. I hold a doctorate in Linguistics.'

'You mean – you can be a doctor and not have to cure people of horrible illnesses?'

'Yes, oh yes, indeed. You can take a Ph.D., that is a doctorate, in your own special field.'

'Oh, I'd like that. I'd much rather be a doctor in a field than win the junior one hundred metres world record, Mr – I mean – Doctor Potter Higgins.'

The door was flung open. Tryphena had arrived.

'Come along, you. Stupid Agnes wants you in the garden.'

I looked back at Theophilus dear, sitting, lost and unhappy, thinking about money as Tryphena hauled me away, bossy cow, then shoved me at Agnes.

Agnes took me into the garden and showed me how she was trying to rig up some sports equipment in *their* shed. It was pathetic. The shed was

rotten and she hadn't got any money to buy things as they were so hard up, she said, and what they had went on musical instruments.

'Wesley, I don't fit in,' she whispered. I nearly told her I wanted to be a writer, really, then I stopped because I wasn't sure I could trust her.

As I left – I'd managed to avoid tea by promising to come back another time for a lovely nettle-soup supper – Mr, I mean, Dr Potter Higgins was waiting for me.

'Come into my study, boy. I enjoyed our little chat last time.'

Agnes was called away to practise, so I entered the book-lined lair again. He showed me a very old book he'd got; valuable, he said.

'Why don't you sell it then?' I asked. 'If you want money for a field.'

'Never, never sell a book. Sell the roof over your head, sell your soul, sell your boots, but never sell a book.'

I couldn't help thinking it would be a good idea to sell the plastic sandals, but I just agreed with the rest. After a while he forgot about me and started looking something up and muttering. I wandered round, loving the old leather books like the ones in my dream. I cleared the cats off a corner of the sofa and found a very old book stuffed down the side. It had a soft brown leather cover with *A History of Dragons, Griffins, Basilisks and all Mythical Creatures* written on it in worn gold lettering. I opened it and there was a picture of MY dragon as I now thought of him. I settled down for a good read.

When I got back home Dad had a new torture in store for me consisting of chin-ups on the beam, which nearly pulled my arms out of their sockets. Then, to improve my general fitness, he made me do laps of the gym shed, vaulting over the horse and the box, climbing ropes and somersaults on the mats. He held a stopwatch and made me go on and on until I could get round the circuit in four minutes. Cliff can do it in two and Rock in one and a half minutes.

Just before I fell asleep I thought that if I could read every book in Agnes's home I could get *really* clever and never, never have to do the circuit again. Then the dragon flew across my eyes flapping his great leathery wings very slowly.

## Chapter Nine

Agnes looked terrible when she arrived at school a few days later. She was wearing a long black dress down to her trainers, with an outsized khaki cardigan and black earrings.

'Looks like a wobbly coming on,' I hissed at Kevin, and hid in the far corner of the room behind a pile of dragon masks in case she wept all over me or something embarrassing like that. Struck by a sudden brainwave, I put one on. It broke. I looked at the name on it and saw that it was Kevin's – naturally. I rummaged a bit and came up with the one I'd made, though I had to squint, because the eyeholes weren't quite in the right place.

I felt safe behind it and wore it till it was time to start maths, and then I kept my head down, trying to camouflage myself as a piece of class-room furniture, and got on with my work.

All was peaceful until suddenly, 'Agnes – you've done nothing at all,' said Mr le Tissier. 'What's the matter? Are you finding this too hard for you?'

'Living's too hard for me!' cried Agnes, bursting into tears.

'Oh, don't cry, Agnes.' Mr le Tissier sounded as if he would join in. He's very soft-hearted. 'Tell me what's wrong and I'll see if I can help. KEVIN, get on with your work. You must not scribble on Simon's plaster in maths lessons. No, I don't care if you were doing a calculation on it, don't do it. Understand? Oh, Agnes, don't cry

so. I'm not cross with you. I just want to find out what's the matter. Come on, Agnes, dry your eyes. Oh, has anyone got a handkerchief? Thank you, Carly.'

'I always carry a handkerchief,' said Carly.

'Wonder your mother doesn't pin it on you like she did when you were little,' put in Kevin.

'KEVIN BREWSTER, get on with your work!'

Mr le Tissier took Agnes up to the desk, where he held her hand and she cried a lot, then she told him how she couldn't play as well as her sisters and so her mother made her practise over and over again and it still didn't come right and Tryphena made fun of her and she didn't want to play the oboe ever again or anything else for that matter. Then she cried even more on to Sir's shoulder.

'Having a great time, aren't they?' Kevin muttered to me, as they whispered to each other.

I didn't say anything. I felt peculiar. Half of me was pleased that Agnes was miserable just like she made me miserable. The other half didn't like seeing her cry. Didn't seem right somehow. I'd got used – well, sort of used – to having her bounce around telling everybody she loved me. Besides, I'd seen her home. Although I liked her father I felt really sorry for her having to practise so much when she hated it. I knew how she felt. Last night I was absolutely finished at the end of Dad's programme. Rock and Cliff had just made fun of me and called me a wimp. No wonder she was mad. And sad.

I tried to go on with maths and not think about Dad or Agnes, but my mind kept drifting to story-writing. You see, I like writing stories. Better than athletics, anyway. My dad came into school yesterday to coach all the kids ready for sports day. I came near to last in almost everything, while Kev and Agnes were coming first all the time. They always do, though neither does any of the things my dad says are guaranteed to

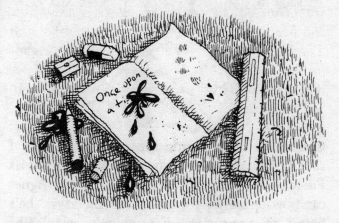

bring you SUCCESS. He's always on about SUCCESS, is my dad. I am a big disappointment to him.

'I knew it was a mistake naming him after that uncle of yours,' I heard him say to Mum. 'A born loser, if ever I saw one, your Uncle Wes . . .'

'He sent a nice christening present . . .' said Mum.

'What's that got to do with it?' asked Dad.

Thinking of all this wasn't doing much for my maths, but Sir was busy with Agnes, telling her how wonderful she was at athletics and she should be proud instead of crying, so I let my

mind drift like a gentle breeze to stories. As I said before, I love writing stories, though Mrs Pooter thinks I copy Agnes. Actually, Agnes can't write stories for toffee. As Sir says, she's better at gymnastics. Everything's crazy! She ought to be my dad's girl and I ought to be with her dad, instead of her worrying about music and me about sport. I'd really love to be a writer or a Doctor in a field like Theophilus dear, surrounded by all those books. Agnes could have our PE equipment instead. All we've got at home are do-it-yourself manuals, *Reader's Digest* and *Healthy Living*. I could even put up with their grot to get my hands on those books. I'm sure a bit of grot's healthy. You should try eating your grub in a kitchen laboratory like ours. Makes you feel like a rat, kept there for experimental reasons: which rat can run the fastest, jump the

highest – yuk. Mind you, I wouldn't be able to put up with Mrs P.H. and the Ghastly Girls for long. They're as awful in their way as Rock and Cliff. I thought of getting them all together . . . hilarious . . .

A story was writing itself in my head, getting between me and maths, not that I was doing any maths anyway.

*Wesley Baker, great hero, wrestles with his bonds in the dark dank cave hidden deep in the treacherous, towering cliffs far, far away on the deserted island, its sands untouched by Man since the beginning of time. The tide is sweeping in rapidly, the wild white horses leaping and surging in the foaming sea, coming nearer and nearer to the rocky opening.*

*Wesley retreats into the back of the cave, his eyes swivelling madly to find a way of escape. But he can see no break in the blackness, no light streaming through a hole to show a way of escape. He seems doomed to perish beneath those stormy waves.*

*But what is that? Above the sea's roar he hears a sound. He rushes to the mouth of the cave. Can it be, can it be? Yes, it is.*

*The sky darkens as the wild sound of beating wings is heard. Dragon is coming. Dragon to the rescue. Dragon swooping towards the cavemouth. And on his back, hair streaming in the wind, is Agnes.*

*Dragon lands her among the seahorses, and she slides from the gleaming scales, runs across the wild shore towards the caves and cries, 'Wes, I've come to save you.'*

*Her earrings sparkle in the strange, weird, eerie, spooky, mysterious twilight.*

*'Wes, don't be afraid. Dragon and I are here,'*
she cries.

SHE? Why was I thinking SHE? And why was
*she* wearing earrings rattling in the wind? Did
Agnes Potter Higgins get everywhere in my life?
I won't, won't have her rescuing Wesley. I don't
want her rescuing me, especially on Dragon.
Dragon's *mine*. Agnes has nothing to do with my
dreams, my writing, my Dragon.

But come on, Wimp Wesley, Agnes is far
more likely to rescue you than the other way
round.

But I can – I can write good stories. I could
write the play of *St George and the Dragon* much
better than Mr le Tissier's done. He's got no
drama in it – no thrill.

'Stop day-dreaming, Wesley, and get on with
your maths,' called Mr le Tissier.

# Chapter Ten

Everything was ready. Dragon Week had arrived at last. Posters were pinned up on the railings outside school and had been pasted all over town. My poster did not win the competition. Penelope, the Child Genius from the reception class, won the Infants, and Sophie Potter Higgins, the Gifted Girl, won the Juniors – well, they would. Lots of copies were made of their posters and sent to the Mayor and all the important people and also placed in our local paper, the *Trumpet and Echo*. The rest of us got nowhere. Mine and Kevin's were on the canteen door, where they didn't last very long.

Mrs Warble, a vision in a rainbow silk dress and golden tights, with golden combs in her hair, talked to us from the platform.

'I know you will all be wonderful,' she called out. 'My dear, dear children. Our Dragon Week will be a wonderful success and a milestone in the History of the School.'

There was a horrible choking noise from the back, and we all swivelled round to look at Mr Clunthorpe, who seemed not very well. His class took him away.

Every classroom had a copy of the week's programme, which went like this:

### THE WEEK'S PROGRAMME

| MONDAY | Morning:<br>Afternoon: | Preparation<br>Mayor's speech in hall. Tour of work |
| --- | --- | --- |
| TUESDAY | Morning:<br>Afternoon: | Plays and songs (Infants)<br>Football match (Heathcliff Combined School<br>v. Farway Community School) |
| WEDNESDAY | | Sports day |
| THURSDAY | Morning:<br>Afternoon: | Plays and songs (Juniors)<br>School Choir and Orchestra<br>– 'Dragon' Symphony |
| FRIDAY | Afternoon: | Play: *St George and the Dragon*.<br>Close of Dragon Week |

'This is a wonderful day,' Mr le Tissier said, as we gathered round. Agnes, dressed in what looked like a purple sheet, was sniffling a bit. She hadn't called out 'Wezzie' or brought me any prezzies lately. Her personality had changed. As the dreaded concert drew nearer she grew

even more miserable. And I knew just how she felt. The thought of sports day terrified me. Sports day would be BLACK WEDNESDAY.

'A wonderful day,' repeated Sir.

'Why?' asked Kevin.

'Because the Mayor is coming to declare Dragon Week open,' said Sir.

'Dragon Bang you mean, Sir,' Kevin called out. 'Everybody's calling it Dragon Bang.'

'Who's everybody?' asked Sir.

'The kids of course. Us. Them that matter.'

'Oh. I didn't know.'

'Well, you wouldn't, would you. But you gotter admit, Mr Tissue, that Dragon Week's a bit weak. Geddit? Dragon Bang's much better. It'll go with a bang . . .'

'Yes, yes.' Mr le Tissier sounded irritable. 'Yes, all right, call it what you like.'

'Mr Clunthorpe's class is calling it Draggy Week, because they're not being allowed to do anything.'

'I don't really wish to discuss Mr Clunthorpe and his ideas. What they do is up to him and his class.'

'No it's not, Sir.' Kevin spoke heavily. 'It's up to 'im. Wot 'e says goes. And I don't think it's fair that they can't join in anything.'

'They will be showing their work like the rest of us.'

'But they won't be 'aving any fun. Like sports, and the *St George and the Dragon* play.'

'I wish I wasn't in the sports,' I put in. 'My dad says he'll be sorry he wasted money on a cup if I don't win something. I keep telling him I won't, but he doesn't get the message. It's hopeless. He'll make me suffer.'

'Perhaps you'll do better than you think, Wesley. And I'm sure your father is happy to donate a prize to someone who has done well.'

'You don't know his dad,' said Simon Partington. 'Well known for being mean is Wesley's dad.'

'Children, children, hush,' called out Mr le Tissier. 'I want to discuss the programme of events with you . . .'

'I think that play is rotten,' said Kevin. 'It's the worst play I've ever been in. Why can't we make it different? I'll eat Agnes and kill ole Wesley 'ere. That'd cheer 'em up and give the parents and guvnors a bit of a giggle.'

'My mother wouldn't like that. My mother's the Mayor, you know, Mr le Tissier, and she wasn't very pleased when you picked Agnes Potty Higgins there for the princess.' Carly tossed her head like a horse.

An extra loud sniffle came from Agnes. It seemed to be Poor Me Week as well as Dragon Bang.

Mr le Tissier had a peculiarly wide smile on his face, so I knew something was coming. He cleared his throat. Kevin cleared his as well.

'Shh,' said Mr le Tissier. 'Now this is important, children. This afternoon we shall all go to the hall, where the Mayor and the Chair of the Governors will make their speeches.'

'Funny, that,' interrupted Kevin. 'I didn't know chairs could talk.'

Half the class told him what 'chair' meant, and then Sir came in with his explanation, after which Kevin said it was all as clear as mud.

'Shush, shush,' went on Mr le Tissier. 'We shall all go to the hall for the opening and then afterwards the Very Important Persons will circulate through the hall and look at your work.'

'Won't take long in my case,' said Kev.

After lunch we all piled into the hall which was decorated with a huge dragon mural. Two large screens were also covered with children's work. In fact, hardly a square inch of the hall was left uncovered. We sat on the floor to listen to the speeches, and Kevin wriggled as if he'd got ants in his pants.

There followed speech after speech. Carly's mum, the Mayor, looking exactly like Carly but wearing a heavy gold chain, spoke loudly and clearly; the Governor Chair, whatever he was, went on boringly for ages, then lots of other people; but at last they finished, so we clapped and clapped and cheered as it was great to have something to do after sitting on the floor for so long.

Later, they all toured the classrooms. Actually, I wanted Dad to see my work. Some of my diagrams were OK.

I heard Sir say, 'Wesley is a bright boy who works well.'

'But what about his athletics?' said my father. 'What about sports and games? I know he can do his work, he gets his brains from me – but he's a WIMP, and I don't think you get tough enough

with him. Plays and poems and art and craft, they're fine in their places, that's what I say, let's be fair, but more importantly, get him to do his maths, spell properly, know a bit of science and learn to win at races. Learn to be competitive. That's what he needs. That's what he's got to do. You must get tough with him. Toughen him up.'

Mr le Tissier had retreated to the corner behind the dragon masks and my dad was standing over him (he's six foot three, my dad) talking to him in his very loud voice.

'I wish I was dead,' I said to the kid next to me. Then I looked at who it was and it turned out to be Agnes.

'I know what you mean,' she said, for Mrs P.H., who had appeared, was now talking at Mr le Tissier.

'I'm not satisfied. I know Agnes isn't gifted like Sophie. Sophie is destined for Immortal Heights and I shall see that she enters Theophilus's old college at Oxford. But Agnes is not

fulfilling her potential at all, Mr le Tissier. You are not working her nearly hard enough. You are too kind to her. She must work harder. Even if she has none of the gifts of my other girls she . . .'

Mr le Tissier managed to break into the flow. Very bravely, I thought, as Agnes and I listened.

'Agnes *is* gifted. But at sports,' he said. 'She is

really very good at PE and games. And she's a very nice girl.'

I thought Mrs P.H. would explode.

'It's her WORK that counts,' she mouthed at Sir. 'Her work and her music.'

My dad joined in.

'I agree,' he shouted. 'All children must work harder!'

At that moment Mrs Warble appeared in the doorway, gleaming and shimmering, surrounded by people gazing adoringly at her.

'I'm so sorry,' she murmured, 'but I'm afraid we must all move on. Time is up. Come along, everyone.'

Agnes and me, we heaved sighs of relief. Her mum and my dad talking to Sir was the Absolute Pits. We walked out of school miserably together, neither of us any good at what *they* wanted.

'I'll come last in my races, Agnes,' I muttered.

'You won't be any worse than me playing in the concert,' she answered.

We stared at one another.

'Come on, Wesley, let's run away from it all,' she cried.

So off we ran, but she soon outran me and, anyway, we couldn't get away from it all, so I turned in at home, ran upstairs and lost myself in the dragon book belonging to Theophilus dear, and wishing he was my dad, until it was Programme time.

# Chapter Eleven

Tuesday afternoon was like sunshine in the middle of a storm. Our team, the Heathcliff Rats, played the Farway Ferrets, that's the school up the hill. Kevin played like a demon, just like Gazza or George Best, and our class was over the moon – he scored three goals and we won 5–2. Kev got carried off shoulder-high, as we sang 'We are the Champions'.

Our class stood together on the field, but at half-time someone pushed in beside me, and even though everybody was watching football, people turned round to look, cos it was Peachey and she was wearing our school kit and the school scarf and boots, and she looked Beeeooooootiful. She'd brought pasties and our lot ate them – we weren't supposed to eat on the field, but Peachey didn't know, did she, and she shouted and roared when Kev did something

brill, which was all the time. Mr le Tissier
couldn't take his eyes off her, cos she jiggled a
lot jumping up and down, and he looked happy
for once. It was great, and I was happy as well,
for she picked me up and kissed me – smack,
squelch – when Kev scored, which caused me to

swallow a huge lump of potato and swede and it
got stuck, but I didn't mind, cos as I say, I was
happy – until I saw Agnes standing there dead
miserable and wearing black.

But I made the most of being with Peachey

and the team winning, because back at home
Dad went grinding on about my not being out
there playing with Kev and wasn't I ashamed
and jealous, and I said, no, I just liked watching
Kev and he was great. And he roared out that I
was a useless wimp so loud that Mrs Nightingale

next door came in and complained to Mum, and
then he said I had to practise for two hours. But
I was still hopeless at the end of it and I cried in
bed cos I was stiff and sore, and I thought again
about running away, but you've got to be brave
to run away, and I'm a useless wimp.

And, of course, he went on and on about sports
day and his hopes for me. Even Mum protested.

'Can't you see Wesley's not equipped for what
you want of him?' she shouted.

Dad shouted and I cried. Then I went up to
bed and lay imagining sports day and me coming
last in everything and Dad . . .

At last I got up quietly and wrote my *own*
version of *St George and the Dragon* and it was
brill, much better than Sir's. My dragon was

fierce and grand and sparky, not like Sir's dreary old reptile. I could see him clearly – as I escaped into my own world, the one inside my head where nothing outside matters – until I fell asleep and dreamed that I was eating apple pie on a beach with Peachey. The dragon swooped in the summer sky. Peachey told me to eat up all my pie and not to be scared of him. But she turned into Dad and I woke up, sweating.

Next day was sports day, BLACK WEDNES-DAY.

'I'm so scared I could die,' I told Kevin. 'It's not fair. You're never scared of anything!'

'Yes I am. I'm scared it might be sprouts for dinner.' And he bent over laughing.

'I think I'll just give up,' I said to Kev.

'Don't worry about things. That's what Peachey says,' he replied.

'It's all right for Peachey. Nobody expects her to do anything except look beautiful and cook.'

Kev rolled about. 'Don't kid your stupid self. Ten As at GCSE, that's what Peachey's got. Taking four A levels.'

'But – but – I didn't know.'

'Kids like you never do, Wez, you old nutter.'

We ran off heats for most of the morning. Dad was there helping with the PTA members, check-ing at the start and finish lines.

He'd entered me for a lot of races, though Mr le Tissier did come and say I wasn't to overdo things. After all, he joked, he wanted his St George fit enough to slay the dragon. I gibbered back. (Thinking of *that* didn't help. The last rehearsal was terrible. Carly and I were the only ones who knew the lines, Kev and Agnes can't act and the costumes and scenery weren't finished.)

At last the awful moment arrived. We took our places on the sports field. The sun shone, lots of people were milling about. Everything and everybody seemed on top form, smiling, happy. Except for me, except for me, except for me.

After the heats were over, I was left in the hundred metres, the fifteen hundred, worst luck – I'd hoped I hadn't qualified for that; I hate long races – the hurdles, the relay and the three-legged race. The last was a joke race, which Kev had entered me for.

'The first race is the hundred metres,' a voice announced through a loudspeaker. 'Take up your positions.'

I could see Dad's face glowing and beaming at the far-away finish as we lined up. This made me sad, knowing I'd soon disappoint him.

At least this race will be over quickly, I thought.

'On your marks. Get set. Go!' The gun fired.

My right foot trod on my left shoelace and I stumbled. By the time I was upright again the rest were halfway down the track. I sprinted after them, to no avail.

I didn't dare meet Dad's eyes as he handed out the ribbons. I could almost feel his thoughts.

After a few other races came the relay. This hadn't gone too badly in the heats. Hopefully this would be better.

I was in the third position, out of four. I waited edgily while the other runners zoomed round the track towards me. Then the baton was placed in my hand.

'Go, Wez,' was hissed in my ear and I rushed away.

Kev was the last in line, being the fastest in the class, and he was pawing the ground impatiently as I headed towards him.

'C'mon, slowcoach,' he growled, and stuck out his hand.

I offered it to him and the baton slipped to the ground. 'Birdbrain,' he hissed at me, and chased after the others. We didn't win.

The hurdles were next. Surely I'd have better luck in this event? If I came home empty-handed there'd be hell to pay.

As the gun fired I shot away, keyed up this time. There were eight runners and I'd had a good start. I was third, then second. C'mon, Wez, I thought, you might win something this time.

Then my leg caught the top of the second from last hurdle and I crashed over, thump, on my chin. I lay stunned for a second, then got up and hobbled over the line – last.

I looked up and met Dad's stare. 'I couldn't help it,' I mouthed at him. 'I tried my best.' It didn't do any good.

There was a short break for me before my next race, the fifteen hundred, which I needed. My chin and leg hurt from the crash with the hurdle and I'd had enough for one day. I wanted to go home. But there was no way out of it.

As the fifteen hundred was a long race it had a staggered start, and funnily enough, I was first on the outside. I wouldn't stay there for long.

I felt rather dazed, waiting there. The day was hotter now and I was tired and dizzy.

The gun fired and I started running, automatically, not concentrating, just wanting to get it over with.

As I ran along, I started to feel dreamy, and then the dragon appeared above me in the sky. The sun shining on my back felt like him breathing on me. He flew above me effortlessly as I ran, dizzily, head and leg aching.

'Dragon, help me. Pick me up and carry me. I can win then,' I pleaded, by now oblivious to everything and everybody else. 'Please.'

Then he flew down and picked me up like a bird catching a worm. I went limp in his grasp.

When I came back to reality I was sitting on the edge of the track, Kev beside me.

'You OK, Wez? You just collapsed halfway round. We thought you might have fainted. Sir was bothered, and he sent me over.'

'Did I?' I asked. 'I can't remember what happened.'

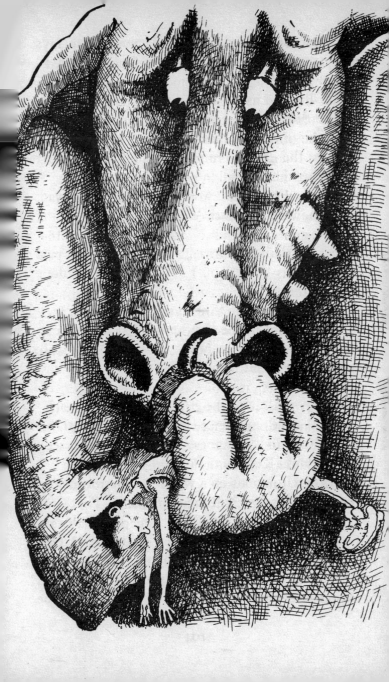

'Your dad looked in a mood. Never mind, it's only the three-legged race now. We'll win it all right.'

'Will we?' I asked. 'I doubt it.'

We did, funnily enough. Kev, fed up with me dragging him back, sort of lifted me up, and we flew to the end of the race, my outside foot just touching the ground.

'Well, Wesley, you won something,' cried Dad, handing us our ribbon. 'But what a disappointing day.'

'Dad, Dad, I'm sorry,' I managed to say to him (I was puffed out). 'But Agnes has done brilliantly.'

'I know,' he said. 'She didn't let me down.'

At the end of the day he handed out his cup for the Sports Person of the Year. But there were two. Agnes and Kevin had tied for the best results.

'They shall have the cup for six months each,' Mrs Warble announced as Dad presented his beautiful cup – to Agnes first (I was glad to see), as he thinks Kev is an idle good-for-nothing.

'Congratulations on a wonderful performance,' he said to Agnes. And then, grinning, 'That's my girl!'

I thought of all the times I'd dreamt of Dad saying, 'That's my boy!' to me, and realized, then, that it would never happen. I looked round to see if her father and mother were there to be pleased as well, but they weren't in sight. Couldn't be bothered to turn up, I suppose. Peachey banged Kev on his back. Then she saw me.

'Oh, Wezzie, you were great.'

'Oh, yes, Wezzie, I do love you,' cried Agnes in front of EVERYBODY except Dad, who'd walked away, not waiting for me. He didn't want to know.

But Agnes said, 'It's all right. I know how you feel.'

Maybe she wasn't as bad as I used to think she was. At least she was sympathetic, whereas Kevin had just stood there grinning all over his ugly mug as everybody congratulated him and Agnes, saying what talent, what talent!

# Chapter Twelve

Thursday morning. We were getting through Dragon Week, and sports day was over. The worst was past, I hoped.

Dad hadn't spoken to me at breakfast time except, 'Don't be late for your practice.' Which meant he hadn't given up on me yet.

As school everyone made an enormous fuss of Agnes and Kevin. People talked of the Olympics. Agnes said she was over the moon, yet she still looked jittery.

'You must be proud, Agnes,' said Sir. 'And your mother.'

Agnes's face clouded over.

'It's the concert *she* cares about,' she muttered.

We were to spend the first part of the morning rehearsing, then we could watch some of the others doing *their* songs, poems and plays later in the morning.

'They're better than us,' Kev said, as we watched the year threes.

I sighed. It was quite true. Our rehearsal had been terrible. Sir's play was feeble, for a start. Now, if we'd been doing mine . . . The dragon in my play, my dream dragon, would have terrified everybody, not lain down meekly and said he was ready to die for St George and England.

That's about as exciting as slaying Baggins, who would roll over and put up with anything Kev dished out to him. No, my dragon would fight and roar and refuse to be defeated. Kev and I agreed on this. Dragons are meant to be horrible monsters, not cosy kittie-witties.

Mr le Tissier heard Kev.

'I do see what you mean. But we can't have too much violence in our play. The Governors wouldn't like it. And don't say that rude word, Kevin, about the Governors.'

'Sir, if you're a writer, you have to say what you think is true, even if people don't like it,' I said, feeling brave. 'It's only right.'

'Sometimes you astonish me, Wesley. And you are right. Well, maybe you can make the dragon more fierce, Kevin.'

He walked off, but then looked round.

'But don't get carried away with it.'

'Huh,' answered Kevin, but it was no use telling him what to do. Kev would do exactly what he wanted, as he always did.

Once more we gathered in the hall. Everywhere buzzed, children giggled, violins tuned up, ping-zing, the tension was high. Mrs Pooter, in black velvet, swanned up and down looking very important.

'Are you still over the moon?' I asked Agnes as she went up to the platform.

'No, sick as a parrot.' She tried to grin. 'I *know* I shall spoil it all, and my mother will be sitting in the front row.'

Sophie sat in the centre of the stage, looking particularly musical. I could see Agnes, dead miserable. I tried to catch her eye and make her grin, but she just sat there, white and trembly.

The 'Dragon' symphony started off. Mrs Pooter bounced up and down, then waved her baton. I can't say whether it was any good or not, but the audience clapped enthusiastically.

Then it was time for Sophie to sing her Warrior Maiden's song. The orchestra started playing and she rose to her feet, her eyes wide, her mouth fixed ready to send out the first note. The audience sat silent, even Kevin.

And a dreadful, hideous, ear-splitting, horrible, discordant wail shredded the air. Somehow Agnes had blown something awful with her oboe, the wrong note at the wrong moment. Time stood still as the entire hall gazed daggers-drawn at Agnes. I looked at Mrs P.H. and she'd covered her face with her hands. Sophie stood rigid, eyes slitted in hatred, while Agnes was white as a sheet, tears raining down her face.

After a long minute, Mrs Pooter rallied, so did Sophie and the orchestra, and the 'Dragon' Symphony continued. Bravely Agnes played on, tears falling, nose running. I felt terrible.

'Good ole Ag,' muttered Kevin.

# Chapter Thirteen

On Friday morning we had the dress rehearsal of *St George and the Dragon*. Kev's costume fell to pieces and we had to mend it. Tim and the rest were painting scenery like maniacs. Agnes forgot all her lines and wept once more. She'd been crying off and on ever since yesterday's concert disaster. Carly prompted her. She knew them all.

'If *I'd* been the princess . . .' she began.

'If you'd been the princess the dragon would've died of shock,' Kev said.

'Children, children,' cried Mr le Tissier, waving his arms. He was wearing his velvet jacket and flowing tie. I liked it.

'It will be all right . . .'

'On the night!' we chanted.

'Except that it's afternoon,' said Guess Who. Everything seemed to take so long as I sat about waiting for Kevin's gear to be mended that I drifted off into my dragon dream. In the bright painted sky flew several dragons. It seemed that they battled with one another and fell to the ground, leaving only the dragon I now thought of as mine. He swooped up and down in great victory rolls until at last he dived down in the deep green valley where his home was hidden.

Kevin's costume looked pretty awful after all. Not that he was bothered. Kev never worries what he looks like.

I think I could've day-dreamed all morning – anything to stop me thinking about Black Wednesday, but suddenly the fire-bell sounded, as if it were raising the dead. BBBRRRRHHHHH.

'Children, children!' cried Mr le Tissier, running backwards and forwards, forwards and backwards. 'It's the fire-alarm. Don't PANIC! Line up at the door. Hurry but don't panic. I must have the register to check you're all here. Where's the register? Where did I put the register? Line up. Hurry! No, don't hurry! Take it steadily. Don't hurry! Hurry! Ah, here's the register. We must make sure we're all here. All here.'

'We're all here, Sir,' said Carly.

'Now, kids, walk out of the classroom, turn left, keep in line, down the corridor, don't get mixed up with Mrs Pooter's class coming up on the right. One, two, three, four, good! Can you keep up, Simon? Wesley, give Simon a hand. Steady now. One, two, three, four. Now turn right and head for the playing field. All together now,' said Mr le Tissier.

Kevin patted Sir.

'I'll look after you, Mr Tissue. And the register. No need to worry. You 'aven't done this before, 'ave you? We 'ave, 'undreds of times. You stay wiv me and you'll be all right. Funny it should be raining though. Don't usually 'ave a fire practice in the rain. We'll get wet.'

'We *are* getting wet,' sounded a furious voice. 'What blithering idiot has sounded the fire-bell on a soaking wet day like this? And in the middle of this ghastly Week? The organization in this school is appalling! Everybody's getting soaked to the skin!' Mr Clunthorpe's voice resounded around the playing field, where all the classes, Infants and Juniors, were lining up in a cloudburst.

'Take care of the registers,' cried Mrs Pooter. 'We mustn't get the registers wet.'

Mr Clunthorpe said some very interesting words about the registers getting wet.

'Where is Mrs Warble?' he shouted.

The playing field was now full of wet children lined up shivering, as teachers tried to check if all their class was present and correct while keeping the registers dry at the same time.

'Where is Mrs Warble?' repeated Mr Clunthorpe. I thought he muttered, 'At her witches coven,' but I might've been wrong.

No one knew where she was.

'Then I suggest we go back inside,' said Mr Clunthorpe. 'Children, back to your classrooms and WALK DON'T RUN,' he roared.

'I shall endeavour to find out why that bell was rung,' I heard him say to Mrs Pooter as they reached the corridor, which was warm and dry, though not dry for long as about three hundred wet children came in out of the rain. It turned out that there was no fire and we'd had no instructions about fire-drill, lately.

'Then there's something wrong with that fire-alarm,' Mr Clunthorpe announced. 'It appears to have rung on its own for no reason. No one went near it. Typical. Probably *won't* ring when there *is* a fire! Hopelessly *inefficient*. Just like this school.'

At last back in the classroom, steaming a bit, we settled down to wet playtime activities and the odd snack.

It was all quite cosy, and we'd nearly dried off, when out of the blue Carly asked, 'Where's Agnes? She hasn't come in with us.'

'Where's Agnes? Agnes is missing!' ran round the classroom. No one knew.

Then Carly said, in a doom-laden voice, 'I knew *all along* that something was UP with her. Agnes has disappeared. I think she's run away. She was very unhappy.'

'She must've drowned,' cried Tim Waring. 'Anyone could've, out there.'

'Don't be silly, Tim,' said Sir. 'She's probably drying off in the cloakroom. Carly, go and look for her all the same. Kevin, you and Tim go and see if anyone's still left on the field. And don't mess about, remember.'

Mr le Tissier pointed at me.

'Wesley, you go and look for her around the school. Try all the corridors and classrooms. Do hurry – we have to find her before the play starts.'

So there I was, wandering through the school, peering into cupboards and classrooms. One class was standing on tiptoe, flapping their arms up and down. Bats, I thought. Definitely batty. I stood in the corridor watching through the glass window at the top of the door till a funny feeling came over me. I looked over my shoulder and there stood Mrs Warble watching me watching Class 5C pretending to be bats.

'Studying school habits, Wesley?' she smiled, making me very nervous. She's got all those wonderful teeth. The only other person with teeth like that is my dad.

'Dud-d-d-d-dud,' I stuttered like a machine-gun.

'Not to worry, Wesley. I do it as well. Very interesting.'

'M-m-Mr le-le Tissier sent me – sent me to look for Ag-Ag-Agnes,' I managed. 'She – she's missing.'

'Ah, I wondered when she'd crack. Can't be easy living with those earrings.'

She walked on down the corridor.

'. . . and that family,' she said over her shoulder.

Then she turned round.

'By the way, Wesley, how are you?'

I felt terrible. What could I say? I thought of sports day and my dad. I couldn't tell her I was hopeless, could I? As unhappy as Agnes, playing her notes all wrong.

'I'm . . . all right . . . Mrs Warble,' I managed. 'Thank you.'

She walked on further.

'Try the hall. Under the platform.'

'Yes, Mrs Warble?'

'Lots of very strange things are to be found under hall platforms, Wesley.'

She turned the corner at the end of the corridor and disappeared.

I pushed open one of the swing-doors into the hall, empty for once. Nobody there. Strange. It's usually full of kids practising or rehearsing. Maybe because it was empty it seemed different, peculiar, or maybe it was just me. What was it Mrs Warble said? Something about strange things being found under hall platforms? I looked at the murals and the mobiles, the screens covered with stories, paintings, diagrams, poems, charts, the half-finished scenery on the platform, curtains pulled back, orchestral instruments on forms in front.

What did Mrs Warble say?

Under the hall platform?

Surely there couldn't be anyone there? Not possible. Just not possible. But Mrs Warble was always right. Everyone said so. Better look.

I didn't like the quiet. It didn't *sound* right. It was exactly like the moment in a film when you want to hide behind the sofa and only look out when you think it's safe.

'Agnes,' I tried to call. It came out like a strangled squawk.

'Agnes, Agnes, Agnes,' echoed all around me. Gulp. I nearly ran. I wished the caretaker would turn up. If he'd walked in I'd've welcomed him like Father Christmas.

'Wesley, get on with it,' I said to me, and ran to the far side of the platform, pushing at each bit of the panelling. Nothing, nothing. It all

appeared solid. Then right round the corner,
almost at the back, half hidden by the dark
curtains hanging above, a little door stuck out
just the smallest bit. I pulled it open and crawled
inside.

'Agnes,' I whispered, and then shut up.

The dark under the hall platform closed down on everything. Then CRASH! Something fell on my head. Darkness reeled round shot with stars as my knees crumpled and I fell. The Black Wednesday races came running through my head one after another, then me losing and Dad's disappointed face. And with Agnes's wrong note sounding in my ears, the smell of smoke in my nose, I blanked out.

# Chapter Fourteen

I came up out of the dark, spluttering and shuddering. Where was I? WHAT AM I DOING HERE? My heart thudded and I trembled. OPEN YOUR EYES, I told myself, OPEN YOUR EYES! And then I realized they were already open.

Something cold and hard and bony, eowh, something horrible touched me. Every hair on my body stood up on end. Oh no – Dad, Mum, Mrs Warble, help me now – PLEASE. With my mouth stuck open in a silent scream, I crouched just inside the little door, too scared silly to move. A cold, bony thing dangled over my face. I shut my eyes tight. Slowly, slowly in the fearful silence I reached out with my hand and touched – ooohhhh – more hard boniness, fingers into spaces, clickety-click. Then I opened my eyes just the smallest, slittiest bit and I *could* see!

I was peering into GIANT TEETH GLEAMING and huge, black, get-lost-in-them-for-ever eye sockets leering down at me. I flattened right down as low as I could go, whimpering for my dad. He'd save me from this terrible monster. What have I ever done?

It's all Agnes P.H.'s fault. Why was I sent after her to die in terror under the hall platform? Mrs Warble, how could you let this happen to me? Sending me under here to meet a SCREAMING SKULL! It's going to get me. I closed my eyes. I'll die in the dark. Oh, why doesn't somebody come? Where's the caretaker? Not taking much care of me, is he?

I looked around. My eyes grew used to the gloom and I could see more clearly, though I could still smell smoke. My head hurt and I rubbed the lump rising rapidly on it. It was very tender. Something had walloped me hard.

I gingerly put a hand forward to touch the object that had scared me so. A skeleton. It dangled, rattling, from a hook, leering at me in the dark. I poked its eye sockets and grinned

back at its grin. Behind it stood brushes, mops, cleaning stuff. It was a storage place down here.

There were also boxes, old clothes and props from old plays. I crawled past a helicopter from *The Flying Postman* and a Narnia lion.

I could see all around me now: strange shapes,

animals, creatures like Dino but much better, a doll's house, a ladder, boxes full of clothes, swords, bits of trees and scenery. I found a stuffed parrot on a stand.

'Pretty Polly, Pretty Polly. Know any swear words, then? Speak to me, Pollykins. Tell me I'm not crazy.'

I made my way through cardboard rocks and boulders that I vaguely remembered from some play or another. Wasn't anything ever thrown away? The history of the school was here under this platform.

'Agnes. Aaaag-neeees,' I called, wobblily.

No answer. I hadn't expected one, but the sounds echoed in a way I didn't like at all. I looked round over my shoulder – not easy when you're crawling – just to check that the little door I'd come in by was still open – for easy escape, something said in my head.

I couldn't see it at all. Smoke curled up from my feet. Behind me stood the shadowy shapes of trees, wolves, bushes. Was that a bear? Cut-out cardboard animals. But no entrance door, no way out.

Instant panic. I was going round in a circle. Lost! I couldn't be lost under the hall platform, surely? Oh yes I could.

I put my hand on a cardboard cut-out of a rock. Only it wasn't. It was solid and it was damp and covered with moss. It was for real. So was the bush beside it. And the trees behind the bush, covered with living green leaves. My stomach lurched in fear.

I swivelled round. I was going back the way I came, back to the little door, the safety of the classroom and Mr le Tissier. But behind me the territory was now completely unfamiliar, grown into a wood of trees, brambles and huge plants reaching to the roof. I tried to crawl through them but they closed up against me, nightmare style. As I sat back on my heels and whimpered, my head hurt. I knew there was no way I could reach the little door leading to the hall and get back to the classroom and safety.

I knelt on moss and brown leaf mould, damp and soft, this mysterious wood all around me, changing and growing until I was surrounded by a forest of huge trees – a forest of olden times such as I'd read about or seen in pictures. Slowly I stood upright, staring, straining to discover a way through, but finding only more trees, catching glimpses of the blue sky above, amazed (and terrified) that all the time I'd been in the school, all those years, THIS had existed under the hall platform and I hadn't known. This enormous, strange, extraordinary world had lain here while kids had gone to assemblies, done sums, had fights, written stories, skedaddled through the ordinary everyday school-things kids do, while here below lay an enchanted forest. It was wonderful, amazing, astonishing, fabulous, fantastical, brill, WICKED; I loved it and it scared me stiff.

And somewhere in that wood must be Agnes, lost, like me.

Then from far away I heard a voice.

'Wez, where are you?'

I struck out towards it through the curling mist.

'Kev – Kev,' I shouted.

'Wez – Wez,' came back like an echo.

Kev was here. Everything would be all right if Kev was here with me. 'Kev? It's me.'

'Wez,' bellowed a voice. 'Come on over here. There's a path.'

Kev suddenly appeared out of the mist and beckoned me. He looked strange, almost transparent.

'Kev?' I warbled at him.

'C'mon,' he bellowed. He started off along the path and I followed.

'This seems to lead somewhere,' he said over his shoulder.

'Kev, what's all this about?'

'Jiggered if I know. But we might as well keep going as stand still.'

We followed the path, which twisted and turned and wound downhill, trees all around us. Kev looked shadowy. I rubbed my eyes, but

though Kev *looked* different he *sounded* like his old self.

'What did the coat-hanger say to the hat?' he asked.

'Oh, I don't know. I don't care either.'

'The coat-hanger said, "You go on ahead, I'll hang about."'

'Oh, stuff it. Everything's bad enough without you making your stupid jokes.'

'It was only to stop you being scared.'

'Well, don't bother. Nothin's gonna stop me being scared. Anyway, I like being here even if I am.'

It grew hotter as we descended, down, down into a valley, mist rising all about us. Kev got up speed and it took me all my time to stay with him. The valley looked familiar. I'd seen it before. I shook my head to try to clear it, but it hurt.

We stepped past a rock that stuck out half across the path. The valley was full of weird shapes and trees. Fog spiralled up from the crevices into beautiful weird shapes.

'They're dragonish,' I said. 'Look, Kev, look at that one.'

'Oh, there are you,' cried a shadowy Agnes, stepping out of a cloud. Like Kev, she was transparent – a little unreal.

'I've been waiting for you,' she said.

Was I pleased to see her!

'Agnes. Oh, great! Wherever did you get to? Why did you run away?'

But before she could answer a wind arrived, whistled up from nowhere.

If I live to be nine hundred and ninety-nine I never want to encounter a wind like that again. Its screech was ten thousand whistles blowing as ten thousand trains collided. Trees and rocks toppled. So did we. We lay behind a huge boulder holding tight to a scrubby little tree with its roots firm under it. Alone, we'd have been blown away, but the tree and the rock held and so did Kev, Agnes and me, clutching each other, deaf, dumb and blind. It felt like it lasted for ever – but it was probably only two minutes.

Then silence came. A stillness you could almost feel after the shouting noise of the wind. At last we could stand upright. We spat, rubbed our eyes and ears. I couldn't speak.

'I'll never moan about maths again,' spluttered Kev.

The path cracked open. Just in time Kev grabbed us as we all sprawled flat behind the rock once more, clutching the little saviour tree. The wind had been terrifying. This was much, much worse. The world shook, rattled, fell apart, broke open, stood on its own head.

'Hold on,' bellowed Kev. 'Just hold.'

The ground rolled, heaved, sank, threw up mud, hurled stones and rocks into the smoking, roaring depths below.

This is the end, I thought.

And everything stopped still, completely still.

The landscape was changed. We stared at red rocks looming high above a deep hole down which stone steps wound their way into the middle of the earth.

'Come on,' cried Agnes. 'There's a path.'

They both held out their hands to me. I could see through them to the rocks behind as I swayed, sick, dizzy, afraid.

'No way,' I cried. 'No way am I going down there. I want school and Sir. I'm not staying here. It's not my scene.'

I tried to run back along the path, but even as I did everything shot up in flames like a car exploding on television. The only safe path away from the roaring, blistering heat was down those purple stone steps. We had no choice.

So down we climbed. Down and down and round and round until we couldn't see the fire any more and it grew cooler. Then, after a long time, the staircase widened, a glow lightened the gloom, growing brighter with each twist and turn of the stairway. Our ears and eyes and mouths eased after their battering as we descended lower, robot-fashion, Kev holding Agnes's hand, she holding mine as I brought up the rear. For ever and ever and ever, as I said.

But it wasn't. The stairs widened, we turned again, the roof rose higher above us as we entered a huge open space as big as the school hall.

There it lay, raised on a stone platform in a deep alcove; coil upon scaly coil; huge, shining; smoke curling gently from cavernous nostrils; gleaming gold and green and scarlet and silver, metallic and armoured. DRAGON, of course,

fast asleep. My Dragon. All around him lay piles
of treasure, surely the greatest hoard in the world:
diamonds, rubies, emeralds, sapphires, gold,
crowns, coins, weapons, armour, cups, daggers,
swords – a dream of dreams.

We didn't dare move.

Then, 'Cor,' muttered Kevin.

Everything swirled about us – me, Kevin,
Agnes, Dragon. I felt so wobbly I was afraid I
might faint. Smoke choked the atmosphere. I
took a deep breath as Dragon opened one huge,
golden eye. At last he spoke in a still, small
voice.

'Welcome, children. Now, tell me your
names.'

# Chapter Fifteen

How do you stop a monster smelling?'
asked Kev.
'I've not the faintest idea,' breathed
Dragon smokily.

'Cut off his nose!'

I watched Dragon nervously. Old Kev's joke
seemed a bit over the top, considering where we
were and who we were with. But Dragon grinned
his nerve-shattering grin, blew six smoke-rings
and uncoiled his tail happily.

He and Kev swapped jokes for some time.
Well, swap's not the right word as Dragon only
knew one – about a dragon crossing the road to
get to the other side. Just about the world's
oldest; very suitable, I suppose, for him. We
were seated on the rock platform where we'd
been throwing for Highest Score with golden
dice set with jewels. Dragon had given us each a
pile of precious gems to start off the game. I was

now left with a handful, Agnes a fair pile, Dragon none at all and Kevin a huge heap he could hardly see over. He and Agnes seemed very happy and not at all surprised. They might have been in school. But I felt very strange. My head hurt and everywhere was still smoky.

We had talked for hours. At least, mostly Dragon talked and we listened. I sat quietly, closing my eyes when everything swirled dizzily around me.

'I am many things. A sea serpent, a winged crocodile with a serpent's tail. I am a guardian of caves, of castles, of maidens, of treasure. I am a mythical beast. I am a legend. I have many names. I dwell as a sea serpent rippling my long tail beneath the water. In China and Japan I fly benevolently through the skies. I am beautiful and I save lives. I am wicked and I kill. I fought Beowulf. I guard Yggdrasil, the Tree of Life. There are those who claim they slew me – St Michael, St George, St Philip and others – even a woman, Agnes, called St Martha – but they

could not slay me. They perish. I live on.'

He turned round and round and settled his tail like a large dog.

'Visitors are welcome. If they do not betray me.'

He slitted his eyes vertically, which was a bit off-putting.

'Why did you come?' he asked at last.

'I came to look after Wez,' answered Kev.

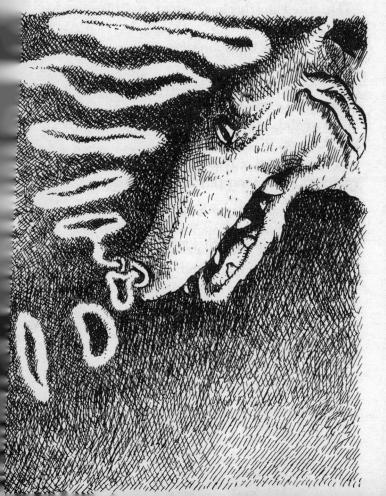

'He's nuts, you see. Like a baby lamb with no fleece on.'

'Oh, I love baby lambs with no fleece on.' Dragon chomped his jaws loudly, smiling. I looked the other way. It wasn't a pretty sight.

'I'm unhappy. I can't please my mum, cos I'm tone deaf and dim,' murmured Agnes.

'My dad thinks I'm a useless wimp,' I muttered.

He lifted up the huge snout and blew twelve smoke-rings.

'Don't be feeble. Don't be unhappy. I'm ME. You be YOU!'

'I told you,' Kev said, boringly. 'Let's just go on with the game.'

So we did, and that's when Kev won nearly all the treasure.

Then we took a rest while we told jokes. All I could remember was this limerick:

There was a young lady from Gloucester
Whose parents thought they had lost her.
    From the fridge came a sound,
    At last she was found.
The problem was how to defrost her.

'What's a fridge?' asked Dragon.

After we'd explained, he turned sad and smoky and his scales lost their shine.

'I don't know about anything,' he groaned heavily. 'I've been alone down here too long guarding treasure and reciting epic poems to the

vampires and lizards. And, y'know, poems like
Beowulf slaying Grendel the monster can be very
depressing from my point of view.'

'You mean, your lot always get done in?' asked
Kev.

'Well, that's what they say. They're wrong.
But I lead a lonely life. A dragon has no friends.'

'You have us now, Draggy,' crooned Agnes,
polishing up some scales with Carly's handkerchief. 'Listen, Draggy. Come up above with us –
if we can get back, that is. You'd love it.'

'Can we take some jewels with us?' asked Kev.

'You mean . . . treasure?' I asked.

'Yeah. Treasure! So I can buy things. Ninten-
dos! Gobstoppers! Trainers! New footballs! A
tiger cub!' cried Kev.

'A tiger cub?' I asked.

'I've always wanted a tiger cub. And a
monkey,' he said.

'What about doing good?' said Agnes.

'You can do the good. I'll have a – mountain
bike, new kit, tons of videos . . .'

'My dad can go on his trip for his research,'
murmured Agnes dreamily. 'And my mum can
have a new dress. And I'll build a lot of homes
and look after all the children . . .'

She astonished me. Maybe Sir was right.
Maybe she *was* a nice girl.

Dragon smoked angrily. He was being ignored
and he didn't like it.

'I want to know what you're talking about,' he said.

'The world above. And school. It's full of YOU,' cried Agnes.

'ME? ME?' asked Dragon.

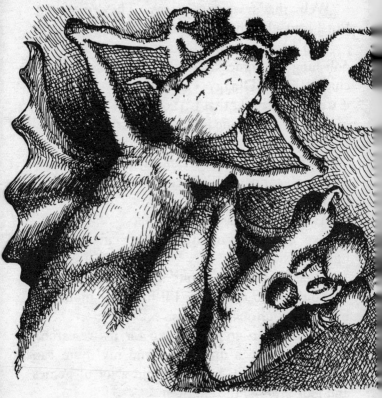

'Oh yes,' she replied. 'Pictures and stories about you and everything.'

'Oh yeah. Wez 'ere slays you, I mean me,' said Kev.

'Slays ME? What are you saying?' asked Dragon.

'Well, I'm St George in our play,' I said, rather timidly, being a bit doubtful about all this. 'And I have to kill you.'

He swelled up, smoking and coiling like mad. We moved out of range of the tail. The friendly atmosphere had altered.

'Look, I don't mean it,' I cried.

'Brrrrhh. Rrrrrhhh. Grrrrhhhh. It won't do. Shameful! Disgusting! No respect! This WON'T DO! Take me to this School place immediately! NOW!'

The tail whipped around angrily. We jumped over it as we tried to get some jewels into our pockets.

'Here,' cried Kev, shoving a Viking helmet on

Agnes's head and a sword with a jewelled handle into my hand.

'Hurry!' cried Dragon. 'I must right this wrong. I must slay St George. I've got to do it all over again. I slew him last time and I must do it now.'

'You've got it all wrong,' I cried.

'No I haven't. History made a mistake. If St George slew me, how is it that I'm still here and he isn't? I've slain all my enemies! Come – come. Show me the way!' Dragon flapped his wings.

'Don't worry. The play doesn't start till half-past one,' cried Kevin.

'Please, please don't kill ME,' I begged, for the dragon was so fierce I felt he was capable of anything.

Dragon snorted and blew out a flame.

'Are we all ready? Let's go,' he roared. 'Get on my back and tail.'

'We'll never get through,' I wailed, but no one was listening.

Dragon's scales weren't slimy and we managed to cling to him as the vast wings spread, flapped and lifted us up, up, up, up into the hall and around, a great flying prehistoric creature, as old as time.

Through the underground hall and up the stone steps soared Dragon, flapping, swooping, gliding.

I was terrified and I was triumphant; it was wonderful. His world slid away: the red rocks, the path. Then we were high over the huge trees of the World Under the School Platform. I was mindless, a flyer in a fabulous dimension; no longer Wezzie the Wimp, but an extension of the flying Dragon, a pterodactyl, a giant bird, the first biplane, a Spitfire fighter, Concorde. Time and space locked together in me.

'It's all one thing,' I cried. 'And me. It's me. I'm it and it's me.'

Where was the world?

I was the world.

The wings decelerated. We flew down, down, down to the world of Dino and props, old scenery and skeletons, down to the World of School.

'I'm coming,' roared Dragon. 'Coming to right the wrong!'

'Don't slay me,' I whimpered.

'How do we get through the little hall platform door?' asked Kev.

'Leave it to me. Magic, of course.' He was smaller, growing smaller. We landed. I stumbled out through the little hall platform door and the billowing smoke.

# Chapter Sixteen

Smoke swirled around everyone on the platform.

'Wesley! Thank goodness you're here,' Mr le Tissier cried. 'We've been looking everywhere for you. Kevin found Agnes ages ago. Everyone's ready except you and we can't do the play without you. Where have you been? No, tell me later. Hurry up now! *Get your armour on, Wesley.* Carly, help him. And have you got the prompt book, Carly? Oh, you know it all? You've known it all, all along? Yes, of course you have. The lights? Are the lights working? Has Mrs Pooter got her music? Simon, have you got the background tapes OK? You have? Fine. Are the onlookers ready? Agnes, you look wonderful. Kevin, you'll do, I suppose. Where's all that smoke coming from? We don't want another fire-alarm. Not with it on the blink. Now, don't panic, don't panic. Just cut down on the smoke, please. I only wanted a bit of smoke for atmosphere, not all that. Wesley, are you ready? What took you so long? Don't panic!'

I wasn't panicking. I moved in a dream, slow speed, as if on hold. Carly helped me into my armour. My head hurt when she put on my helmet.

'You've got a huge lump,' she said.

'I know. But where's Dragon?' I asked. 'He's disappeared.'

'Wez, what are you talking about?'

I stood in the Viking helmet, holding the huge shield and the gleaming sword. Kev shot up in front of me.

'I found Agnes, Wez. Where did you get to?' he asked.

'You know. You and Agnes were with me. But where's Dragon? He wanted to be here.'

'What you talkin' about, nutter? *I'm* the dragon,' said Kev.

'Are you all right, Wesley?' asked Sir. 'You look hazy.'

'So do you, Sir. It's so smoky, it's difficult to see. And, Sir, I must tell you about Dragon.'

'Not *now*, Wesley. Later.'

I could hear people talking far away, sounds from the other side of the curtain. The audience was arriving.

The orchestra tuned up. Quietly music began to play.

I felt very strange. What was happening? What *had* happened to me? My brain ached with trying to remember . . . remember . . . the world under the hall platform . . . curling smoke . . . the way through the woods . . . the wind, earthquake and fire . . . the underground hall and DRAGON.

My dragon who'd haunted all my dreams ever since we started to get ready for Dragon Week and my dad had wanted me to WIN, to be TOP. Oh, my head hurt.

But where was Dragon now? He must be somewhere among all the smoke that was getting steadily thicker. Didn't people notice?

It was hard to breathe. Dragon, where are

you? I'm ready for you now. I've got my armour on. I know I've got to fight you.

Sir was chaining Agnes to her rock. The on-lookers gathered on one side of the platform. The other, a smoky dark corner, was the Dragon's cave. Was he waiting there? Behind Kev? In that dark corner? The music was playing loudly now. Sir pinned a red cross on the front of my armour.

'Are you *sure* you're all right, Wesley? I can get Carly to . . .'

'No, it has to be me,' I said.

'All right, then. We're nearly ready. Good luck.'

'I'll need it, Sir,' I said.

We waited. The music grew louder. Mr le Tissier ran round the stage, hands waving like windmills.

The music stopped. Silence fell in the hall. NOW!

In front of the curtains Carly spoke the Prologue to the audience, setting the scene for telling the tale of long ago which Dragon said was all wrong and he would change. I'd got to stop him. It was my task, for I was St George. Carly's voice rang out:

'With that they heard a roaring hideous sound
That all the air with terror filled wide
As they the dreadful Dragon all espied.

'Then next, the dreadful Beast drew near
                                    at hand
Half-flying and half-footing in his haste,
His body monstrous horrible and vast.'

Carly stepped back from the curtains, ready to prompt from the rear. Eerie music sounded. The curtain rose. Silence fell in the hall. And up through the stage floor Dragon arrived: beautiful, wonderful, terrible, wicked. Himself. MY Dragon!

The onlookers began their chant.

'Come forth, St George, for the sake of our

fair princess and for all of us and for the safety of our land, we beseech you.'

'Come, St George, and fight this fearful beast. Come forth, brave knight, and slay the Dragon.'

Dragon almost filled the stage. This was him, my real, live Dragon. Smoke swirled around us.

'You're not going to kill me!' I shouted at him. 'St George always slays the dragon.'

'What's going on?' hissed Carly. 'Wesley, you're not doing it right.'

'Phew! It's hot!' cried someone, somewhere.

Smoke poured from the gigantic nostrils as we glared at one another across the stage.

'Wesley's messing it all up,' wailed Carly.

'Save me!' shrieked Agnes.

Carly howled, 'Your lovely play's ruined, Mr le Tissier. And I can't see cos of all this smoke!'

'What's going on?' shouted someone in the audience.

'I wish I knew,' cried Mr le Tissier, hands waving. 'Children, children.'

'Get on and slay the dragon!' shouted the onlookers on the stage.

'Slay the dragon!' shouted the audience.

He swelled to full size, nearly filling the stage. He roared, and jetted a giant plume of smoke into the hall.

Somebody in the audience screamed, 'Fire!'

Mr Clunthorpe shouted, 'I knew it. Ring the fire-bell. I knew there'd be trouble.'

'Let me out of here!' shouted a voice.

'Return to your dragon cave,' I cried. 'For I am Wesley, the dragon slayer.'

The sword gleamed in my hand, its jewels as bright as the fire now blazing on the platform.

I could hear Mr le Tissier.

'Off the stage, children! Get off the stage!'

'Wesley's gone mad,' shouted Carly.

'He always was,' yelled Kevin. 'Get him off!'

'Fire, fire!' Screams and cries and running feet.

'Get off the stage, everyone! Come on, Wesley. Wesley, come on.'

'I must slay the dragon before he destroys us all. My dad would want me to be brave and save you all.'

Far away I could hear Mrs Warble.

'Keep very calm. Parents, children, file out in order through the doors. Children, remember the fire-drill. WESLEY, GET OFF THAT STAGE!'

But Dragon roared again.

I held the heavy sword high in my hand – the treasure sword from the cave. I bore down with it on to the great wide jaws: Dragon's jaws.

Like the wild stormy seas in my stories, foam spurted, spraying, splashing over everything, covering everything till I couldn't see at all.

Someone was carrying me out. It might have been Mr le Tissier. It might have been my dad. I didn't know. What I did know was that I'd slain Dragon.

# Chapter Seventeen

I opened my eyes warily. Then shut them. Not a good idea to open eyes.

I opened them again. Mum was there.

'That's better,' she said. 'Good boy.'

I went to sleep again.

Next time Rock and Cliff were with her. Something was up. They don't normally sit round my bed.

'How's our hero?' grinned Rock.

'And what a hero,' grinned Cliff, but not sending me up.

'Why have I got white hands?' I asked, waving them, then not. They hurt.

'Bandaged hero.'

'Wounded warrior.'

It seemed a good idea to sleep again.

Next time I came to I knew I was in a hospital

bed. A nurse inspected me. She looked like Mum.

'Feeling better?'

'Can I go home?'

'Not yet. Soon. Look at all the things people have brought.'

There was some fruit, chocs (but Dad wouldn't let me eat them), magazines, cars, books, books, books and more books.

'Somebody loves you a lot.' The nurse held up a huge card with an enormous heart on it. 'What a lovely old-fashioned girl she must be. Agnes is a lovely old-fashioned name.'

'Hey – what happened to me?'

'You stopped a school burning down. Didn't you know? Got hold of a fire extinguisher and put out the flames.'

'Oh, did I?'

'Yes. But the doctor said you wouldn't remember as you're concussed as well as getting your hands burnt and smoke in your eyes. You're a hero, Wesley. Go to sleep, now.'

There *was* something. I knew. Something about fighting a dragon. I slept.

Mr le Tissier brought cards and letters from school.

'Brave boy. We're proud of you.'

'What did I do?'

'Stayed on stage putting out flames while everyone else got off.'

'Kevin? Agnes?'

'They're fine. Jumped off just before you did. Don't you remember?'

'No.'

'Nothing at all?'

'Dark under the hall platform. Smoke. And something about a dragon.'

'They think the fire started under the hall platform.'

'It wasn't me!'

'No, no, no. No one thinks it was you. But they're investigating it now. Some combustible material under there apparently. Or a faulty light fuse. You mustn't get worked up, Wesley. Here's your mother now.'

She stroked my head.

'Go to sleep, Wesley. Get better soon. We all miss you at school,' Mr le Tissier said as he left.

I slept.


Peachey brought me strawberry jelly in a little dish.

'Kev won't come. He hates hospitals. But he's got a white mouse for you. I said it ought to be a lion, you're so brave.'

She kissed me; oh wow!

'Your temperature's up again. You can't go home yet,' said the nurse.

Mrs Warble came with a huge bunch of grapes.

'My St George,' she smiled, and kissed me. Oh!

Mr Clunthorpe brought lemons for fresh lemon juice; his favourite, he said.

'That fire was smouldering away while we were doing fire-drill, Wesley. Very strange. And there was a loose wire in the fire-alarm. But, good boy. Full marks for getting hold of the fire extinguisher. I'm pleased someone else in that school has some sense.'

Everyone in the ward looked up. The nurse stared. I looked too, and there was this enormous film-star-type man striding towards me with a huge bunch of flowers. I looked again and realized it was Dad. Cor, that's my dad, I thought. I've never really seen him properly before.

He sat down, and everyone tuned in as he boomed, 'Nobody can accuse me of not learning by my mistakes, and I got you all wrong, Wesley. You tried to tell me and I didn't listen. Well, when you come out it *will* be *different. This* is the new routine.'

Oh no, I thought, not again.

'I've been talking to Dr Potter Higgins, who thinks highly of you, and when you're better you're to go to him three nights a week for reading and study and all that, while Agnes comes to us for workouts. We're making up her programme now. She's got a lot of potential. But then, so have you, my boy. Here she comes. She'll tell you all about it, so I'll be off as I don't like sitting about, as you know. Goodbye, Wesley. We'll see you home soon. Hi, Agnes. We'll see you too.'

At the door he turned, smiled, waved to me and bellowed, 'That's my boy.' I could hear a nurse telling him off for whistling so loudly.

'Hi, Wesley,' said Agnes. 'You look happy, even in those bandages.'

'About that dragon, Agnes . . .'

'No, not again, Wez. Don't go on about it. I don't know about any dragon. Only the play. Let's forget it. Isn't it wonderful? Now you can spend time with my dad and I can do my athletics instead of playing wrong notes all the time. Oh, I do love you, Wezzie.'

Much later, perched in the tree-house, finished at last, and stroking the little white mouse with his red nose and soft little feet, I asked Kev about the dragon.

'What dragon? There wasn't any dragon, only me. You've been making up your batty stories again.'

'But . . . it seemed real . . .'

'Oh, belt up. Just live for now, Wez.'

So I did. Belt up, I mean.

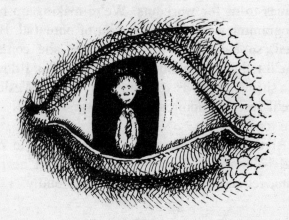